This is Joseph McNair ⬚ ⬚⬚⬚ ⬚⬚⬚
though his poems and s⬚ ⬚⬚⬚
in several literary maga⬚ ⬚⬚⬚
he now lives in Balti⬚⬚⬚
daughter.

Some reviews of *Taking Off*:

"Told . . . in a humorously original style . . . the charac-
terisation is on the mark. An exceptional début." *Kirkus*

"An engaging and touching novel." *School Librarian*

"Lively, absorbing . . . amusing." *Junior Bookshelf*

JOSEPH McNAIR

Taking Off

Piper Books
PAN MACMILLAN
CHILDREN'S BOOKS

For Lois

First published in the United States of America
under the title *Commander Coatrack Returns* by
Houghton Mifflin Company, Boston

First published in the United Kingdom 1991 by
Macmillan Children's Books

This Piper edition first published 1992 by
PAN MACMILLAN CHILDREN'S BOOKS
A division of Pan Macmillan Limited
Cavaye Place, London SW10 9PG and Basingstoke
Associated companies throughout the world

1 3 5 7 9 8 6 4 2

© Joseph McNair Stover

ISBN 0 330 32275 3

Printed in England by Clays Limited, St Ives plc

•1•

"Are you prepared for launch, Commander?"

Cody gives me one of those rolling-eyed looks that signals his readiness.

I remove all of the jackets, coats, hats, scarves, umbrellas, and even a roller skate, until the brass coatrack in our front hallway is bare. Then I lift it up and let Cody crawl underneath. He's gotten to be kind of big for the rack at five years old, and I have to be careful when I set it down over him.

The top of the rack is straight, with little hooks coming out the top for all the stuff I mentioned to hang on. But about halfway down, where there is a second set of hooks, it starts to flare out into four legs surrounded by a hoop. This makes it pretty sturdy, and you can pile on clothes and hats until it resembles an alien that's trying to look like one of us but can't quite decide what to wear. In fact, on the expedition with the roller skate, that's exactly what it was.

Anyway, because the legs bulge out, there's room enough for a small person to fit inside. Cody can't crawl between the legs, he never could. I always have to lift it up and let him get in his curled-up, blast-off position and then set it over him. Then I load all of the clothes back on and begin the countdown.

". . . seven, six, five, four . . ."

Cody makes a sound in his throat, letting me know the dinkles and the astrofarbs are in their pre-fire positions.

". . . three, two, one . . . IGNITION."

Cody makes the sound of the rockets firing, only to anybody else he sounds like an air raid siren going off. I used to try to make the right sound for him but he just got scared, so when Commander Coatrack takes off, it's to the tune of the city's Civil Defense warning.

"Lisa! I'm on the phone." My mom is calling from her bedroom. The launch of the Commander frequently brings notice from the surrounding countryside.

"Commander, standard orbit has been achieved," I say, and take my fingers out of my ears as the noise of his rockets dies down. I'm not sure if Cody understands exactly what I'm saying, but by now we've got it worked out so that there's an order to things.

"Lisa, I've got to get to the store before your father gets home. I promised him that for once dinner would be on time, but here I am running around again at the last minute."

"I can do it for you, Mom."

"I know you can, honey, and I appreciate your offering. Again. But remember that your father and I are trying to work things out so that there's no burden on you."

2

It didn't used to be a burden on me, but now it is. According to Dr. Barnes. That's just one of his brilliant conclusions that I don't buy. He's supposed to be helping my folks deal with Cody, but all I see is him messing everything up.

"If the car doesn't start today I'll scream," Mom says, in a hurry and sounding tired. She takes her coat from the rack and starts to put it on. Immediately Cody starts making a "boop-boop" sound inside the rack.

"You've removed one of his heat shields, Mom."

"Well, I'm sorry, Commander. It's only the end of February and I need this heat shield to keep me warm between here and the store. Hey, I made a funny, didn't I?"

She looks pleased with herself and I give her a smile to make her feel good. She and Dad are having it kind of rough these days, as usual. But she won't let me help out the way I've done in the past.

"I won't be gone long. If your father calls, tell him I'm busy or something. Don't tell him I'm at the store."

"You want me to lie?"

"Of course not. But I can't let him know I'm not keeping to our schedule again." Another of Dr. Barnes's brilliant ideas. He thinks if they can organize themselves on the outside then they'll be able to organize on the inside. Meaning inside their heads. But with Mom standing there staring at her scarf as though she can't remember what it is, I have to have my doubts.

"So what should I tell him?" I ask.

"Tell who?" Mom's still trying to figure out the scarf.

"If you don't want me to lie, what should I tell Dad when he calls?" I ask.

3

"Don't answer the phone, then."

"What if it's an emergency?"

She stares up at me. Her face is kind of twisted funny. I've seen it happen a lot this past year. When the pressure gets too great for my parents, especially my dad, they get these blank looks on their faces and can't decide what to do.

"I'll handle it, Mom," I say. "Don't worry."

That snaps her out of it. "Well . . . good. Thanks." She sighs. "I should be taking lessons from you on how to handle things." She throws the scarf back onto the rack. "Wish me luck." She goes out the door.

I hear the car door slam. Then it slams again. She comes back in. "I can't leave. I'm waiting for a call from a potential buyer. I don't have my head screwed on straight today."

Mom is a real estate agent. I used to think that meant she showed somebody a house and then they bought it, but it's turned out to be more than that. It's not just my parents but *all* grownups who can't make up their minds about things. Including houses. Mom will show the same people forty-three houses and they end up buying the first one they went into. Then Mom sits around with aching feet, her dress smelling of old cigarette smoke — neither of my parents smokes — asking me why she ever wanted to do this.

She used to be a secretary at my old elementary school but thought she wasn't getting enough fresh air in there. She chose real estate because that would get her out in the wide-open spaces. What usually happens, though, is she ends up trapped in her car driving forty-five minutes one direction, forty-five minutes another, with a couple of chimneys in the back seat trying to give her lung cancer. I've told the Com-

4

mander we might have to perform a rescue mission on Mom. He seems all for it.

"I'm sorry. Can you go for me, Lisa? Here's the money. I need the stuff on this list." She gives me all the paperwork and I stick it in my pocket.

"Commander, we're about to make a foray in the space pod. Repeat, this is an unscheduled search-and-retrieve mission to Zondar." Cody understands I mean the grocery store and he lets us know the mission is acceptable by making a happy noise, which sounds a whole lot like his rocket engines firing.

Together, Mom and I can lift the rack off him without stripping it of all the coats. Cody crawls out and we set it back down. "He's getting a bit big for sitting under there," says Mom. "Don't you think you should come up with another game?"

"Mom, you know this is his favorite. His day wouldn't be complete without it."

"Well," says Mom, getting that look, as though she thinks she knows a little more about it than I do, "Dr. Barnes seems to think Cody could stand a little change." She wants to say more but she doesn't.

"Mom, don't you think Cody would let us know if he wanted to do something different? Huh, Cody?" Those last two words I say to him with a special tone of voice, so that I sound almost mad, as though I'm blaming him for something. His face squinches up and he starts to cry.

"Now, Lisa, you're deliberately provoking him."

"Zondar! Zondar!" I say to him and his face lights up. He loves to go to the store. "See, Mom, he knows what he likes."

5

Mom just shakes her head, which means she gives up. It's getting harder and harder to get her to do that these days, though. I think that's because of Dr. Barnes, too. The Commander and I may have to go on the rescue mission sooner than I thought.

I strap Cody into his stroller and push him out the front door. He's almost too big for that, and I've had to break off the side rails to give him room. He can walk okay, but he's easier to manage like this, and he gets a kick out of steaming past other little kids on trikes and wagons and stuff when I kick in the afterburners for him.

"Brace for asteroid belt," I say, and slowly bounce him down the front steps. "Shields holding. Conditions nominal." I'm going to be an astronaut when I grow up. I've got pictures of Sally Ride, who was the first American woman in space, on my walls. By the time I get old enough we're going to have shuttle missions going to the moon and maybe to Mars. I want to get in on that. Maybe by then they'll be letting people like Cody fly up too, and then he'll finally be a real Commander, and he'll sit alongside me as we dock at a space station and float off hand in hand on some great galactic exploration.

At the Mighty Mart we go through the electric door. "Entering Zondar's atmosphere. Hull temperatures rising." We sail past people putting bags of groceries into their carts, about to wheel them out to their cars. I have to swerve to miss a customer and Cody shouts "Wheee!" as I shoot him into the fruit section. Then I put on the brakes again to steer carefully around a wall of canned corn. They set up those walls so that you almost have to run them down. It's the store's way to get your attention, otherwise they'd never sell any of the lousy things.

Hidden behind the corn, I reach into my pocket and pull out a laminated cucumber. We have this cucumber because at one point Mom was trying to dry out gourds for decoration. But they kept rotting. She tried to dry different types of gourds, weird kinds that she had to drive to the city for, but they all rotted too. Then she went kind of berserk and started drying anything she could get hold of, grapes, tangerines, watermelons, determined to make a hollowed-out shell of *something*.

The only thing that worked was this cucumber. Well, Mom was so pleased she set it all by itself on the dining room table for everybody in the neighborhood to come by and gawk at. But there aren't too many interesting things you can do with one cucumber and after a while it got boring to see it sitting there. So she started placing flowers around it, tying bows on it. At Christmas she had a little sleigh with Santa and reindeer riding down it as though it was some big hill of green snow. Anyway, when she finally got tired of the thing I took it off her hands.

"Commander, here is your laser. Be prepared to fight off any Zondarians who may try to thwart us in our mission." Cody is crazy about that cucumber. And it's held up real well, longer than any of his plastic guns. I don't know what Mom did to it, but it's taken a lot of abuse and still looks fresh out of the garden. She ought to be proud.

We cruise around the aisles pulling off the stuff on Mom's list and stacking it all on Cody's lap. He holds it in with one hand and keeps the cucumber at the ready in his

7

other. We are almost finished when a Zondarian launches a surprise attack.

A woman with enough food to feed herself, her husband, and a pet elephant pulls up alongside Cody. At first she behaves like any other normal shopper in a grocery store, but then she gives Cody the once-over and has to say something.

"Isn't he a bit big to still be in a stroller?" Then she looks again. "Oh." She starts staring at his face, memorizing it so she can tell her husband and the elephant what he looks like when she gets home. "What's wrong with him?"

"There's nothing wrong with him," I say, and I can't quite keep from sounding mad. So then she gets this really understanding look on her face that makes me want to throw up and says, "I see."

That does it. When she moves off I give the order. "Prepare to attack. Laser at full intensity." Cody knows what that means, too, and, boy, is he itching for a fight. I wait until the lady is almost at the other end of the aisle and then I back all the way up to my end. Meanwhile, Cody is charging his laser, making little electrical noises with his mouth. "Begin the attack!" I say, loud enough for the lady to hear.

When she turns she sees me racing full tilt down the aisle, pushing Cody, and he's got that wicked cucumber laser stretched out at the end of his arm, making a new sound, like "Pazzuh! Pazzuh! Pazzuh!" Well, the lady must think she's about to be skewered by a large, laminated vegetable, so she screams and bolts around the corner, which is really all we want to make her do. After all, if we cornered her in the cereal section, with Cody sitting there harmlessly going

"Pazzuh! Pazzuh!" she'd eventually go get somebody to throw us in jail. So, at the end of the aisle, with nearly everything checked off on Mom's list, I peel off from the attack and slide right up into an empty check-out lane. Since I have ten items or less I can avoid the other lanes, which are packed with shoppers who were dumb enough to think that Zondar wouldn't be crowded this time of day.

On the way home the thought of that lady is still bothering me. What if it had been my mom pushing Cody around? These days she might do okay, but a couple of years ago she would have lost it. How would you feel if you were taking this medicine while you were pregnant that later turned out to be bad for the baby? How would you feel if the kid came out not looking quite right and not thinking quite right? You'd feel guilty, that's what. And then if some stupid person walked up and asked what was wrong with your kid, wouldn't you feel even worse?

When Cody was born I guess I was too young to understand what was going on. My parents were upset and I couldn't really see why. He was a little more quiet than some babies, and his face was a little different, but he was just another kid to me. And he was my brother. I went in to his room and talked to him and played with him. What could be easier?

I kept expecting my parents to get the hang of things, to start treating Cody the way they treated me. Instead, they just stayed upset. Eventually, Dad decided he needed to stay late at his office a lot, and Mom had a sudden, overwhelming desire to join all of the volunteer organizations in the world, leaving Cody alone with me and a sitter most evenings.

Don't get me wrong, Mom and Dad have never ignored him or anything. They love him and all that, but they just can't stop thinking that Cody didn't have to come out the way he did, that they made a mistake. And every day, whenever they look at him, they're reminded of that mistake. Sometimes that reminder hurts so much they can't stand to face him, to be around him. Sometimes it gets so bad they can't even stand to be around other people, even their friends. That's when Mom and Dad go off the deep end, into a really bad depression, so I not only look after Cody but after both of them.

When it comes to guilt, grown people really know how to pour it on themselves, like thick fudge on a sundae. I can understand Mom and Dad having *some* guilt, but this is ridiculous. Instead of catching on to how really great a son they have, they've let the guilts get so bad in their heads they don't go away. They think too much about how things aren't totally perfect instead of how nearly perfect they are.

Anyway, there was always somebody to clean house and watch Cody through the morning and early afternoon, boring him to tears until I got home from school. And from then until bedtime Cody was mostly mine, since Mom and Dad were usually out until late. This last year or so my parents even let me send the sitter home so that I could take care of him without any busybody interruptions. I mean, nobody knows Cody like I do, so who else was better qualified to show him a good time? And that's how things stood.

Until now.

10

Now Mom and Dad have their stupid schedule.

You see, they started to feel guilty about *me* because they thought they'd sort of dumped Cody in my lap. They thought that I'd start to *resent* them because I had to look after him so much and that I'd be traumatized and grow up hating life and, I suppose, turn cranky and gray before I reached the ripe old age of fourteen. Really ridiculous.

So, my parents decided they really needed some outside help — to scrape off the fudge. A couple of months ago they made an appointment with this doctor, and now they see him every week. But the first thing this jerky doctor told them was that they needed to change the routine around at home, that one of them ought to be waiting at the door when I get out of school in the afternoon, that both should be home in time for all of us to have dinner together, and that they should stop going out so much in the evenings. All this is supposed to "re-establish the family unit." That's what the doctor calls us, a "family unit." You'd think we were part of this giant computer or something, made up of all these other "units" of moms and dads and kids.

Now the great routine Cody and I had going for us is all screwed up. Mom and Dad keep popping into the room where Cody and I are with their hands in their pockets and this look of "what-do-I-do-now?" on their faces.

One problem is that the doctor is having them do stuff they've never done before. For instance, last week Dad tried to cook this meat for dinner. Dad ordinarily uses a stove about as often as I eat frogs. Which is never, by the way. He was trying to broil a steak when I came into the kitchen and had the drawer under our electric oven pulled out and all the pots and pans Mom keeps in there sitting out

11

all over the floor. He was all set to put the beef in the drawer.

"Dad," I said, "What are you doing?"

"I'm going to surprise your mom."

"You sure are. You're going to surprise her with a raw T-bone." He frowned and said he'd seen it done this way once on *Cooking for Klutzes* or some such stupid program. I explained to him that since this wasn't a gas oven the heat for broiling came from the top and not the bottom. He didn't believe me until he put the oven on BROIL, opened the oven door, and saw the wire in the roof turn cherry red.

I guess it's good that my parents are out there trying, since that's supposed to help them act the way they did before Cody was born. But I can't help feeling sometimes that Mom and Dad are in the way.

When I get home from the store I lug Cody backwards up the front steps and go into the house. Mom comes blazing out of the kitchen and I try to figure out real quick what's wrong.

"The Mighty Mart called," she says. And then I know. "Lisa, you're too old to be doing that anymore."

"I was just teaching that lady a lesson."

"You weren't teaching her anything. All you did was scare her. All you did was get your revenge."

"But she was rude to Cody."

"I don't care what she did. You're not going to make people any more understanding by chasing them through a store. If you can't behave I won't let you take him with you anymore. As a matter of fact, he's too big for that stroller anyway. I'm going to get rid of it.''

I know she can't be serious. She can't take away one of the Commander's few joys in life.

''Unstrap him now and help me take everything into the kitchen.'' She grabs a few things out of Cody's arms and starts to walk away. Over her shoulder she says, ''Those buyers never did call me back. I should have gone to the store myself.''

I think Mom likes her job, despite the smoking chimneys and the people who never call back. On top of wanting to get out of being a secretary she needed to earn more money. Cody's had to have operations over the years to correct his insides, and while he's pretty much okay now in that department, my parents are still paying off a lot of bills.

''Sir, we are in protective custody, now. You must surrender your laser.'' Cody hands over the cucumber and I stash it before Mom sees it and has another fit. The first few times we got in trouble, people in the Mighty Mart complained that Cody was carrying a weapon. My mother couldn't figure out what they were talking about until she realized the ''weapon'' must be the one and only vegetable she's ever successfully dried out. She almost took it away from us then, but Dad didn't want to see it on the dining table again with Santa, so she gave it back.

·2·

I like school. I know that when a thirteen-year-old says that, it tends to make grownups grab their chests and drop dead from a heart attack, but I really do like it. I have to like it if I want to be an astronaut. I have to do really well in my science courses plus make decent grades in everything else. The only thing I don't like about it is that most of the other kids there get on my nerves.

I'm pretty much a nothing at school just because I'm smart. Hey, I'm not a genius or anything, but when I get called on to answer a question in class I get it right often enough to get ribbed by kids. I probably would get picked on less if I ribbed them back, but instead I always blush and get tongue-tied and turn away. That sort of behavior has not only got me labeled as a brain but as a brain who's a snob. And nobody is attracted to someone who's a brain and a snob and who also rates about a −4 on the beauty scale.

It used to bother me, but I've decided it isn't worth it. I've got Cody, so who needs anybody else? Besides, when I

14

look around me, what exactly am I missing? The opportunity to join in with kids who think that the ability to drink Diet Coke through straws poked up their noses is a milestone in human evolution? Who think the best way to show affection is to shoot the rubber bands off their braces at people they like? Forget it. I'd rather sit by myself and think about the adventure with Cody I went on yesterday, or plan for the one today.

Another thing that bothers me about the kids at school is that they like to watch television, which I think is the worst thing anybody could ever do.

I know saying something like that also makes adults keel over. But the fact is, television rots your brain. And I probably wouldn't have found that out if it hadn't been for Cody. See, Cody may have trouble in some departments, but he's real perceptive. About people's moods. About their true personalities. More so than ordinary people.

For instance, once my dad hired a plumber to take out a toilet that liked to hiccup and overflow, usually in the middle of the night, and replace it with a new one. When the man came to give an estimate, Dad liked him right away. He was friendly, dressed the way a plumber should, and he was cheap. As soon as he came to do the job, though, Cody cried and cried. Nobody understood why. When the plumber tried to play, Cody nearly bit him. Dad apologized and was real embarrassed. Until he got the bill. The guy charged twice what he said he would. And it was as though Cody'd known that all along.

"Next time somebody offers me a bargain," Dad said after that, "I'll just hold Cody up to their face. If he tries to chew off their nose, I'll know better than to trust them."

So, anyway, about the television. Cody never really noticed the TV his first few years. I figured there were too many other things going on in his life, such as learning to walk, for him to give it much attention. But when he got old enough to sit quietly for long periods of time and take in the world around him, I thought that was the greatest development. He'd be able to see things that I couldn't show or tell him about. But the first time I plopped him down and made a big production out of turning on the TV just for him, a funny thing happened. He started to cry, the way he did with the plumber. He looked at the screen for a few seconds, then cut loose. I thought maybe it was just the show — it was a Western. I thought it was too violent or something so I turned the channel. The next thing we saw was a friendly guy doing the news. Would you believe it? Cody started crying even harder. I flipped through all the channels. We saw cartoons, soap operas, exercise shows, even Mr. Science, who was my favorite. Cody hated it all. He wouldn't settle down until I turned it off.

The only reasonable explanation I could think of was that Cody found something really wrong with watching television. It was affecting him in some kind of bad way, being the type of sensitive kid he is and all. So I figured, well, if it's bad for him it must be bad for me. So I stopped watching it.

As time went by, I started noticing how often kids watched television. That was all they talked about sometimes, as though that's all that was important in life. It explained a lot of things — intra-nostril Coke sipping, rubber band romances. That's how I decided TV rots your brain. I couldn't believe I used to watch it myself. And with the time I had left over from *not* watching TV I discovered I could read science magazines and books I used to think I never had time for.

I've tried to convince people at school about the mistake they're making, but they won't listen. They are too far gone. They have A.T.B.R., advanced television brain rot, and they can no longer understand what a normal person may be trying to say to them.

My best friend is Vandelle Barnsdorf — a lot of kids make her mad by calling her "Barn Door" because she's a little wide. She's my only friend except for Cody. Actually, I think she's my friend more than I'm hers. She's a very independent person and more or less just lets me tag along with her.

She lives near me and I've known her since first grade. She helps me entertain Cody sometimes but she's never been real big on little kids. She's more interested in hanging around and talking with my parents. She likes them a lot and whenever they've gotten to feeling especially torn up over Cody, and coping with them has gotten too much for me, I've always been able to go to Van. She's usually able to calm me down and come up with the answers to my problems.

I remember one time Dad was so depressed that he stayed in bed for days. I couldn't budge him, and Mom was content to leave him there. Meanwhile, Dad's office kept phoning, wanting to know where he was. I was going crazy not knowing what to do, so I told Van and she set the azalea bush in the front yard on fire.

That might sound like an unusual way to go about curing a depressed father, and the fact is when I first told him about the bush he didn't believe me and just stayed where he was. But then he smelled the smoke.

The neighbors have some interesting pictures of Dad in his underwear holding the garden hose, and I sort of think the whole thing has had some effect on his opinion of Van. But, like most of her plans, it worked.

So I guess what I'm saying is, I just couldn't have made it through without Van. She's been like an older sister, even though we're really the same age. And on top of everything else, she's never owned a television.

It doesn't matter to me that her parents just never bought one. The point is that she's gotten along fine without it, and she thinks other kids who talk nonstop about TV shows are as far gone as I do.

Van is interesting not only because she doesn't watch television and sets bushes on fire, though. She's ahead of her time in many ways. She went punk a whole year before it became fashionable in our school. Out of the blue she came to school one day with her hair dyed green and strings of paper clips in place of earrings. She had on a white plastic trash bag for a blouse that said MEGATRASH across the back, and it had holes ripped in it so that you could almost see her breasts and red paint streaked down the front like blood. Her pants had rips in them, but they were held together with safety pins. On her feet she had these nasty-looking imitation leather boots with spike heels and a pair of snow chains from her father's Volkswagen wrapped around her ankles. No one in the whole school was anywhere near dressed like that. I'd never have had the guts.

She got sent home right away.

She came back the next day with a note from her parents asking if their daughter was doing badly in school or if she was in any way harming other students. Our principal, Mr. Mann, is not very good with confrontations — he's more concerned with whether the student council is taking more than their monthly allotment of dittos or whether too much money is being spent on athletic equipment — and he had to admit that Van was one of the best students in the school. And since there is no strict dress code in the student handbook, he had to let her back in.

Van calls her parents Liberal. My dad calls them Transplanted Backwoods New Money. He says that the first summer after she learned to walk her parents used to let her run around naked outside and use the trees bordering their side yard as a bathroom. When the next-door neighbors complained, Mr. Barnsdorf explained that this was how they potty-trained children where he came from in Georgia. He said that Van would get used to relieving herself without messing up her clothes, so that when she had to wear them again the next winter she wouldn't want to ruin them. Van is proud of the story and calls her parents' reasoning "advanced thinking." My dad calls it something I'm not allowed to repeat.

Van is also the smartest person I know. She wants to be a cultural anthropologist. She believes that a long time ago, before history was written down, the world used to have a matriarchal society, which means women ran everything. She wants to travel around the world looking for evidence that this is really true and then throw it in the faces of all the hot-shot men who run the world now. She also wants to see if she can find where those women went wrong, how they lost control of everything. I've backed her all the way. Until lately.

"If we can only get some top posts in the government, we'll be able to fix the world," she tells me.

It was just yesterday that Mom decided to doom Cody's stroller to the trash pile and I'm still upset.

"Women don't know everything either, Van," I say, slamming my books inside my locker.

"Shhh!" she says. "You don't want the ENEMY to hear things like that." Van doesn't like boys. They tease her about being kind of fat and also about being kind of big up top. In fact, once when Cody was with me over at her house he picked up one of her bras, put one of its cups over his head, and it fit.

"That's not a good attitude to have," she warns me. She's playing with the end of a hangman's noose she's wearing like a necktie today. Actually she's getting tired of going punk. There is now a bunch of kids who go around looking like Van. She doesn't associate with them, though. Like I said, she stays ahead of the times.

"We've got to hang together," she says. "What's so funny?"

"You're saying that with a noose around your neck," I say, laughing at her.

"Well, you know what I mean." She doesn't think anything is funny where the matriarchal society is concerned.

"Van, why are you talking that way?" Sometimes she's hard to understand because of the southern accent she's inherited from her parents. She's spent almost all of her life here in Ohio, but her voice is thick with a Georgia drawl, in part, I suspect, because she enjoys sounding different from everybody else. Today, she's even worse than usual, as though her mouth is so dry she can't open it very wide.

"What do you mean?" she says, knowing *very well* what I mean.

Just then some of the ENEMY walk by, a group of four boys who have always been particularly rude to Van. Jimmy Pinto is the leader.

"Hey, Barn Door, how come you're not out planting cotton?" says Jimmy.

"Maybe she's afraid if she bent over the weight would make her fall on her face."

They all laugh and wait for her to say something. Van usually handles herself pretty well, but this time even I'm surprised.

She steps back away from them, like a gunslinger at high noon. Only instead of whipping out her six-shooter she just stands there, and very slowly, very *very* slowly, her tongue comes out of her mouth. Now, you wouldn't ordinarily think that sticking your tongue out at somebody when you're past the second or third grade would be much of a comeback, but right in the middle of Van's tongue, in living color, is the picture of an eye. I don't mean just a little drawing either. It is a masterpiece. With eyelashes and everything. One big eye, just staring down those four jerks.

Well, of course there's not much you can say to a girl with a noose around her neck and an eyeball on her tongue, and those boys just walk quietly away, occasionally glancing back at us.

21

"Quick, let's get to the bathroom," says Van, just as soon as they've turned the corner.

"What have you got that on with? It's beautiful!" I ask.

"You wouldn't want to know," she says. "And I'm beginning to wonder if it was worth it. Do you know I've waited all day to do that? I haven't had a thing to drink since I put it on, so it wouldn't smear. My throat is so dry I'm surprised my tongue didn't stick in place. Come on."

In the rest room I have a chance to think while Van is busy scrubbing off her eye. "You know, you really ought to stop doing stuff like that."

"I don't do all that much."

"Uh-hunh. You don't see me going out of my way to annoy people. If somebody gives me a hard time I just pretend they're not there."

"For the good of our sex we've got to stay on the offensive."

When Van says "sex" I blush, even though I know she means "women." I'm afraid to tell her that lately I've been dreaming about having a boyfriend. I think Van would croak. Either that or put the noose that's around her neck to good use on me. There's not much chance of me dating, though, because the boys here aren't interested in me. Just as well. I think most of them have the rot real bad, and I could never go out with somebody who has A.T.B.R. That would be like dating Cody's cucumber.

"How's that look?" Van sticks her tongue out at me. Most of the eye is gone, but there's still a sort of smeared shadow, as though the eye were now looking out from behind sunglasses.

"It's fine," I say.

22

The bell rings and we hurry to Mrs. Cronski's history class. Van has a real problem with this class because she feels that Mrs. Cronski should dwell more on the accomplishments of "our sex" in history. But Mrs. Cronski just goes by the book. What's worse is that she practically faints when she talks about generals who were real macho during wartime. Van wants to puke when that happens. It's as though Mrs. Cronski used to be married to them or something, as though her last name used to be MacArthur. I've seen *Mr.* Cronski and I can understand why Mrs. Cronski would wish her last name really was MacArthur.

Van's noose draws some attention, but everybody's pretty used to the way she dresses by now. We sit in the back of the room where Van can keep an eye on things. Sometimes she likes to put her feet on the seat and her rear up on the backrest of her desk and lean against the wall. Mrs. Cronski used to get after her about that, but Van called her bluff about getting Mr. Mann down here — he hates to come into a classroom unless he's figured out a way to cut back on the amount of chalk teachers use or something — and so she leaves her alone.

After the bell rings and everybody is reasonably quiet, Mrs. Cronski says, "Class, we have a new student joining the school today. Robert?"

This kid I hadn't noticed before stands up by the pencil sharpener and turns around.

"This is Robert Wormer," says Mrs. Cronski. That gets a few laughs and she pretends not to notice. "Would you prefer to be called 'Bob'?"

"Charles."

Mrs. Cronski looks at him. "Pardon?"

23

"I'd prefer to be called 'Charles.' "

Mrs. Cronski looks down at his transfer papers and must read over them bout fifty times, trying to find the name "Charles." Finally she says, "But there's no . . ."

"Or 'Charlie,' if you want." Then he sits down.

Mrs. Cronski looks at the transfer papers again and must wonder if she's got the wrong student. Finally she just tucks them away in a little folder, acting as though she isn't really concerned and gets on with the lesson.

Robert Wormer, a.k.a. Charles, a.k.a. Charlie, doesn't impress me much one way or the other. He looks like an average kid and acts like one too, except for having trouble with his name. I can't tell if he's got the rot, though. I'll have to get up close to him and look into his eyes. A person with a bad case of the rot has eyes that sort of shine when the light hits them a certain way, as though they've become two television screens all their own. Van thinks it's just because most of the kids I've looked at closely wear contact lenses, but that's her opinion.

Van slips me a note. "Another member of the ENEMY admitted to campaign against us. The administration strikes again." I write back, "They don't have any choice about who they let in here. It's just by chance that he's a boy." When Van reads that she gives me a look, as though I've just tightened the noose around her neck and cut off the air supply. Her mouth hangs open a little and the eye on her tongue peeks out at me with the same disbelief.

After class Van and I have to go different ways, and I end up behind the new kid and a couple of the guys who bothered Van this morning.

"Hey, Worm Hole," says Jimmy Pinto. These guys are real creative when it comes to playing with names. "I've got a rotten apple for you to crawl into."

If I were this new kid I would just keep walking. Jimmy is mean and he is dumb. The two together make him dangerous to be around. He once got into a fight because he thought he heard somebody in English class call him an oxymoron. He was held back a grade, so he's bigger and stronger than his cohorts and that's made him the boss.

But Robertcharlescharlie doesn't keep walking. He stops dead in his tracks, so suddenly that Jimmy and his buddies almost collide with him. I stop, too, and the five of us cause a little logjam in the hallway.

What happens next is kind of hard to describe. First of all, Robert turns around. Then his arms sort of float up, making me think of a giant puppet with strings attached to the elbows. When his arms are up high, curving out from his shoulders, he speaks.

"I am . . . a bird."

That's all he says. "I am" with a little pause, and then "a bird." I can't believe it. This new kid is flipping out in the middle of the social studies hallway.

Jimmy, as always, is prepared for anything strange to happen. He says, "What?"

"I am," Robert says again, slowly, "a bird." And then his arms start to move up and down a couple of times, like a big bird flying.

"Well, I don't think they allow animals on school property," says Jimmy. That gets a few laughs from his buddies, but Jimmy looks confused.

"There are certain organizations designed to take care of people like you," says Robert, sounding an awful lot like Mrs. Cronski when she's mad at somebody.

"And there are rooms with padded walls designed for people like you," says Jimmy. He's used to dealing with Mrs. Cronski.

"I told you. I'm not a people. I'm a bird."

Then I see that Robert's not flipping out. He's just putting Jimmy on. And Jimmy is having a little trouble figuring that out.

"So where are your feathers?"

"Under my clothes."

"Hey, Jimmy," says the guy next to him, trying to help out, "why don't we take off his shirt and see if there are feathers on his chest?"

By now a crowd has formed to check out all the excitement. Jimmy gets this grin on his face. "Let's see if he's got them all over."

By this point, though, the bell has rung and there are teachers staring at empty rooms, which is not supposed to be the case in a school. So they start wandering out to see where all their students are. Mr. Hummel, another history teacher, is the first to elbow his way to the middle of the group.

"All right, what's the story?" Mr. Hummel looks as though he should be teaching shop. He's big and keeps his sleeves rolled up all the time. He has hairy arms.

"Nothing. Nothing at all, Mr. Hummel. Does it look like there's anything wrong?" Jimmy puts on his innocent act and looks at Robert for support. It's an unwritten law that kids will back each other up when it comes to fending off teachers and administrators.

"He was blocking my flight path," says Robert. Jimmy's smile collapses into a little pile of ugly wrinkles and he scowls at Robert.

"Well, the runway to the principal's office will soon be clear for landing. How would you like me to put you two in a holding pattern in the waiting room?" That gets a few laughs, and I think Robert figures he's gone about as far as he can without ending up facing Mr. Mann.

"All right, let's go. Let's go," says Mr. Hummel, shooing people away, although most everybody scattered when he first appeared. Robert and I get left standing there by ourselves. I know I'm late enough as it is, but I just have to say something to him. I've never seen anybody but Van stand up to Jimmy Pinto before.

"You were great," I tell him.

He looks me up and down with eyes that I can now see are deep brown. There's not a trace of A.T.B.R. in them.

His eyes look right through mine, wander around inside my head, checking things out. Then he walks away without saying anything.

Wait until Van meets *him,* she'll *have* to change her mind about guys.

+3+

When I get home from school Mom and Cody aren't home, but Dad is.

"Where is everybody?"

Dad looks up from the kitchen table where he has all these jars spread out. "Mom took Cody in for some tests."

I've heard those words before and I feel the hair on the back of my neck come to attention. "Is Cody sick?"

"No, no. She's just taken him in for some intelligence tests."

I finally start breathing again and my hair returns to its naturally flat and unattractive shape. I can't get my hair to do anything I want it to. I'm allergic to perms and if I roll it the curl stays in for all of an hour and a half.

Once I thought about shaving it all off and going punk, but Van talked me out of it. She said that I'm so skinny that with a bald head the police would think I was dead and try to get me buried — Van is not too subtle sometimes. My parents said if I went through with it I wouldn't just *look* dead, so I gave up on the idea.

I sit across from Dad and start peeling an orange. "What's he need to take more tests for?"

"These are different types of tests," Dad says. "We should be able to get a better idea of what he's capable of learning. You want him to live up to his potential, don't you?"

"Oh, sure." I imagine Mom dragging home, disappointed again. They ought to just leave him alone. I don't really have a whole lot of faith in I.Q. tests, anyway.

Once when I took one in elementary school I just chose the same answer for all of the questions. Boy, did that mess people up. My parents were called in for a conference and had to persuade the administrators not to put me back a couple of grades. And the principal had a stroke, yelling that I couldn't *do* that on I.Q. tests. I think they need a separate scale, to rate those of us smart enough not to take it all so seriously.

Dad gets up and starts rooting around in the silverware drawer for a spoon. He's pretty intelligent, for a father, but he's the type that's never quite tucked in. No matter what he does there's always something wrong with his clothes. Today his tie is out of his shirt collar and his shirt tails are hanging down outside the back of his suit jacket. Mom used to safety-pin Cody's shirt tails into his pants when we'd go to church and has recently threatened to do the same thing to Dad.

Dad sits back down and removes the lids from the row of jars, then takes a yellow legal pad and makes columns down the front page. When he's through with the columns he digs the spoon into the first jar.

Dad's degree is in agriculture and chemistry. In the lab

29

where he works they worry about growing farm crops that can stand up to disease and bad weather and still taste good. His specialty is peanuts. In fact, he's been working with peanuts for so long that just by eating one he can tell where it was grown. Peanut butter companies from all over are always sending jars of their latest brands for him to sample and give his opinion on. We have shelves full in the pantry. On his days off, like today, he takes the time to open up a carton or two.

Have you ever watched a movie where some rich guy opens up a bottle of wine that has an inch of dust on it and then goes through this whole routine of looking and sniffing at it in his glass for about five years before he ever takes a sip? That's what Dad does. Except he does it with peanut butter.

First he digs the spoon into the jar, then he holds the sample up to the light. He says he does this to study the texture, but I think he's looking for bug parts. Then he sticks it under his nose and gets a good whiff. Finally, he eats it, writing down on his legal pad whether it's bombed out or not.

He enjoys these taste tests and I suppose I should be proud that he has this unique gift. Unfortunately, when lunchtime rolls around at school I can usually bet on what's going to be in my sandwiches.

I hear the front door open and Mom comes in with Cody. "Hello, hello," she says, one hello for each of us. She gives Dad a kiss on the cheek and he gives her a goose on the rear end. I can't believe he still does that. It's embarrassing.

Cody straggles in behind. Dad picks him up and gives him some peanut butter. Cody just sits there, zonked out. I've seen this look before. I've seen it in the mirror after *I've* taken a test. I've also seen it on the faces of kids with A.T.B.R. and I'm convinced that it's a similar type of brain damage.

"How did it go?" asks Dad.

Mom puts a hand to her forehead, as though she's having trouble holding in everything she learned today. "He tested well. He's . . . he can start going to that special school they've started there in the hospital."

Mom might as well have said she'd decided to become a cannibal and we were having our neighbors, the Dentons, for dinner tonight. I look at Dad, who's looking at Mom.

"Really?" he says. "Why that's . . . sooner than we expected — hoped — isn't it?"

"Cody can go to school? When did you guys decide that?" I still can't believe it.

"Well, we haven't . . . yet. We agreed to have him tested a while ago. But I guess we have to decide now whether or not to go ahead and enroll him." She looks at Dad, who smiles, and Mom nods back at him, smiling as well. Then Mom turns to me. "What do you think, Lisa?"

I don't know why, but something unpleasant clicks in the back of my head. "Hey, I think it's great," I say, and I do mean it. But my voice doesn't come out sounding too enthusiastic. Mom seems to be relieved as soon as I say it, though. "What's he going to study? I mean, how is it different from a regular school?"

"Well," says Dad, "there's a lot more physical therapy

31

involved, a more intensive effort to develop coordination. And then the cognitive learning, the thinking type of learning, will be very basic kindergarten work.''

I turn to Cody and see that he has the look of somebody who hasn't slept in three days and isn't going to function too much longer. "Well," I say, getting up, "it sounds great to me," still not sounding completely wholehearted. "I think I'll take him upstairs right now and help him unwind." I gather him up out of Dad's lap and carry him toward the kitchen door.

"Careful, now," says Mom, "he's getting a little heavy for you."

"I've got him," I say, although it is a little like carrying a forty-pound meat loaf up the steps. I take him into my parents' room and set him on a chair, with his legs going up the back, his back on the seat, and his head hanging upside-down over the edge. Sometimes this helps. It calms him down and gets the blood flowing back to his brain. Now he looks like a real astronaut about to take off, with his feet pointed toward the universe.

Why is that easier to imagine than him in school?

I can't think any more about it right now; it's made this fog roll in on my brain and I need to clear it away by doing something else.

I pick up the phone and punch Van's number.

"Don't stay on too long," calls my mom.

I don't know how she does that. She can be asleep in the sun in the backyard and still wake up as soon as I go for a phone. Funny how when kids hit puberty their mothers are suddenly able to hear every dial tone, swear word, and opening of the refrigerator door.

"Hello?"

"Hi, Van. What do you think of the mysterious Mr. Wormer?" Even the news about my brother hasn't completely shaken him out of my thoughts. I'm hoping to get Van to say something nice about him.

"Who?"

"What do you mean 'who?' The new kid today in class."

"Oh. Why?"

"Because I think he might be a good recruit for our battle with Jimmy Pinto."

"First of all, Jimmy Pinto is just one of many to be made to see the light. Secondly, you don't fight fire with fire, no matter what they say. You use water. And the women of the world together form the vast ocean that's going to extinguish the wildfire of male supremacy."

"Are you reading that out of a book?" I ask.

Van sniffs. "No-o-o," she drawls, "it's from a speech I'm preparing to give between A and B lunch periods in two weeks."

"Since when?"

"Since this afternoon when I asked Mr. Mann if I could use the stage in the auditorium and run off a few flyers on the office mimeograph machine to put up around school."

"And he said yes?"

"Yes. If I promised not to turn on the lights in the auditorium and brought in my own ditto paper for the mimeo machine."

For the second time today I have an uneasy feeling. "Aren't you afraid of making people angry?"

"Democracy cannot advance on the two left feet of men. There must be the equally balanced steps of women to lead the way so that the world can march, left, left, left right left, into the future. I wrote that, too."

I have to sigh. "Well, *anyway*, can I tell you what he did?"

"What who did?"

"You're not listening to me!"

"Lisa, I'll listen when you start to make sense."

Sometimes Van thinks that I'm her reflection. She just starts talking to herself, like she's looking into a mirror.

"Van, look, I'm trying to tell you about the new guy." So I tell her what happened between Robert and Jimmy and then wait for some sign of approval.

"He sounds very strange," she says finally.

"What?"

"Acting like a bird. Pretty bizarre, wouldn't you say?"

"I can't believe you. Who painted an eye on their tongue today?"

"That was a specific, calculated, well-executed plan of action. This guy all of a sudden went nuts."

"You're just determined not to like him, aren't you?" I say, getting mad.

"Why? What difference does it make? Say, do *you* like him or something?"

This is a moment I've been dreading for some time, admitting I'm interested in boys. But this has all come about unexpectedly. I don't even *know* this guy and he's already getting me in trouble. "Maybe I do," I say. And, because I never have been able to persuade Van about anything before, and because it's so hard sometimes to get her to take me seriously, I say something kind of stupid. "Maybe I'm in love with him."

"You're what?"

I can imagine Van looking into her mirror and seeing a crack starting to run up it. "You heard me," I say, although my voice is so faint I can barely hear it myself.

There's a long silence on the phone, and for one wild moment I imagine that Van's dropped it, grabbed a knife, and is now running over here to murder me. But then I hear her soft, southern sigh and she says, "When you snap out of it, give me a call." Then the line goes dead.

I stare at the phone, realizing what I've done. I've just chased away my best friend. And for what? The phone makes its little dull note. The sound is very empty, and lonely.

I hang it up and hear a giggle. I turn around to see Cody still upside-down in the chair. The position seems to have helped. His eyes are moving around and his hands are poking at the air. His cheeks, though, are a little too much on the red side.

"Oops, guess I forgot about you." I turn him around and the color in his face goes back to normal. I kneel down and give him a hug. "Cody, I think I did a very dumb thing with Van. But you won't hold it against me, will you?"

"Pazzuh!" he says, and I don't know if I'm getting shot or if he's saying it's okay.

I take him downstairs to look for something to do now that he's revived. We pass by the den and Dad is in there with the television on. I glare at him.

He sees me and pleads, "Lisa, it's PBS. It's educational. It's not that bad."

I just shake my head and walk on. In the kitchen Mom is pulling together the odds and ends of dinner. I sit with Cody at the table and make him a sandwich. Cody can eat and eat without getting fat. He'll eat a full dinner even after this sandwich, so Mom doesn't mind. Sometimes after a really big meal, when Cody is still calling for more, Dad will get down on his knees and put an ear up to one of Cody's legs, then the other, tapping with his knuckles as he goes. "Looking for that hollow leg," he'll say. "There must be a hollow leg where all that *food* goes."

Mom says over her shoulder, "How is Van?"

"We aren't speaking."

"Since when?"

"Since ten minutes ago when she hung up on me."

"Oh." Mom goes back to chopping celery. "Can I help?"

"I think we're beyond help. It's a basic attitude problem. She believes one thing, I believe another."

"Sounds very serious."

"It *is*, Mom. Don't make fun. She's my only friend."

"I'm not making fun," she says quietly. "And I know she's your good friend." She lays down her knife and looks at me. "But she shouldn't be your only friend."

"But she is. She's the only person worth anything in that whole school."

"A lot of parents would be distressed to hear that."

"You *are* making fun."

"I'm sorry. I'm just wondering if you aren't being awfully hard on twenty-four hundred teenagers. I'm sure a few of them could find an extra friend in you."

"Not likely."

My mom folds her arms and leans back against the sink. Then she looks at the floor. "Isn't there any kind of science

36

club that meets after school? Wouldn't those kids have something in common with you?''

"What's the big deal? I can live without Van." Although I'm not sure I can. "Besides, I can't get involved in stuff after school. I have to get home to Cody and help him have some fun.'' I look at Cody, who's chewed his sandwich into the shape of a gun. He lets Mom have it, then me. "Pazzuh! Pazzuh!" Then he sticks it in his mouth and bites off the barrel.

"You know," Mom says slowly, "I've said for a while now that with our new program you don't have to rush home." When Dr. Barnes gets tired of saying "schedule" he substitutes "program."

Mom adds, "Dad and I have gotten fairly good at entertaining him.''

"But Mom, I *like* being with Cody. And he needs me around. I'm his best friend.'' As soon as I say that it hits me that Cody's a lot like me. That each of us only has one friend in the world. And now mine is gone. That makes me sad and mad again all at once. "I wouldn't desert Cody the way Van's deserted me.''

With that Mom leaves off bugging me about having other friends and gets back to Van. "Oh, Lisa, I can't believe she's *deserted* you. I'm sure it will all pass over in a couple of days.''

You just can't expect a parent to understand. I change the subject. "Do you want help with dinner?" I ask.

"No, no. I'm fine. I'll get it all." Mom trying to be independent again. "If you have a strong desire to be constructive you can get some homework done before we eat.''

"Okay." I take Cody by the hand and lead him away

37

from the kitchen. When we pass the den I look in again. The television is on but Dad is not. He's in his chair with his eyes closed and his head rolled over onto his shoulder. Just more evidence for my case. I go in and turn the TV off and go up to my room.

I get Cody situated with a game and then stretch out on my bed with my math book. I open it up to the lesson, but I can't concentrate. The numbers all turn into a foreign language, like Chinese or something, and refuse to make any sense.

I can't decide what's more important, keeping Van as a friend or being able to get married some day. Actually I'm kidding myself. Van will come around. Some day. Maybe. But right now she's just got this thing going about boys and I don't know what to do about it.

And what about Robert Wormer? Does he even know I'm alive? The way he looked at me and then just walked away sure wasn't very encouraging. But there's something about him.

Maybe I'm just attracted to weird people.

That isn't a very pleasant thought. Weird people might turn out to be something more than weird. Like *crazy*. Is that what's wrong with Robert? Is he really a psycho? No, Mr. Mann may be a pretty poor principal, but I don't think he'd let a basket case into school. Or would he?

All of a sudden I get a picture in my head of Robert Wormer dressed in a feathery bird costume, flapping around the neighborhood looking for a victim to fall prey to his poison-tipped beak. Then I picture Van chasing after him with this human-sized birdcage, trying to get him inside and shouting that the bald eagle was chosen as the national bird out of discrimination, because only men ever go bald.

I sit up on the bed with the beginnings of a winning headache. I look over at Cody.

"Pazzuh!" he says.

"Thanks. I needed that," I say, and drop dead back on the bed.

✦4✦

The next few days at school are depressing. I would feel the same way if, suddenly, when I went home every afternoon Cody wasn't there anymore.

During the times when I usually go hang out with Van I don't know what to do with myself. I want to apologize. Tell her that I love good books, and blue skies, and peanut butter — well, maybe not peanut butter anymore — but that I don't know anything about loving a boy. I don't think she'll listen, though.

In history class she just ignores me, or she'll look over at Robert Wormer and then back at me and press her lips tightly together. I feel like a kid in a new school, having to get used to everything all over again.

To top things off, Robert hasn't done a single interesting thing since the other day. He's a different person. Mrs. Cronski has settled on calling him Robert, not Charles or Charlie, and he hasn't given her any trouble about it. I start to think I've made one terribly big mistake.

One day I wander down by the music room. It's at a time when I'd normally be at Van's locker cooking up a way to liven up Mrs. Cronski's class, to make our dear teacher see the shackles that bind her, et cetera. So I go down there to get as far away from Van's locker as possible.

I'm not very musical. Once Mom tried to get me to take cello lessons. Most mothers would try to get their kid to take piano lessons, but not my mom. She got the idea in her head that if I started with an unusual instrument that I'd grow up to be an unusual person. I think I have, but not necessarily in all the ways Mom would like. Anyway, I took cello lessons from a Mr. Graveston. He was about a hundred years old and never bathed. He was always reaching around me from behind to show me how to draw my bow across the strings. It was like being wrapped up in a big smelly blanket that you couldn't escape from. I tried to tell Mom, but she just thought I was being ungrateful about being given the opportunity to grow up into this unusual person she had pictured in her head. So one day when the smell was really bad, when he had his mouth opened wide enough to let me know that he also hadn't brushed his teeth that day, I bit him on the wrist. Mom was mad but she didn't send me back, not after Mr. Graveston refused to accept her apology and made a crack about having to go to the hospital to get rabies shots.

As I walk by the music room I hear an unusual string of notes ring out, almost like wood chimes being nudged together by a breeze. I step in to see what's making those sounds, and there is Robert Wormer. At first it looks as though he's standing behind a table; then I see he's got some kind of mallets in his hands and that the table is an

41

instrument. I freeze by the door. He doesn't notice me and starts to play his table.

With his brow furrowed in concentration, he takes his mallets, two in one hand and one in the other, and races back and forth. I see that the table is made up of wooden blocks, and each block makes a different note, and when he strikes several blocks at the same time they make a chord. He's very good, and the music is wonderful. It makes a picture in my head of a bunch of people chasing each other around, bumping, falling over each other, and when they finally stop and dust themselves off, they start the confusion all over again. Finally, it all comes to an end, with everyone collapsing in one last big heap.

"You were great," I say, without thinking.

Startled, Robert looks up at me. When he sees who it is he relaxes and looks at me the way he did in the hall the other day. "You said that before," he says.

"I guess I did," I say timidly, walking a little into the room. "I suppose that means you're just an all-around great guy."

I can't believe I've said that. My first real conversation with a guy and I say something to embarrass both of us. The only thing is, Robert doesn't seem embarrassed. He just cocks his head and looks at me, the way somebody in an art gallery studies a statue after suddenly noticing a crack in it. That's how I feel right now, as though my brain's got a crack in it.

"What was that called?" I ask to try and cover up my stupidity.

" 'Galloping Comedians,' " he says.

"You're kidding," I say. "That's just what I imagined

as you played. All of these funny people trying to get somewhere and do something, but they just kept running into each other." My smile fades when Robert keeps standing there, staring at the crack. "Coincidence, hunh?" I say weakly.

He straightens his head. "Not really. That's what it's supposed to evoke."

"Evoke." He used the word "evoke." You don't hear anybody with A.T.B.R. using a word like that. I start to like him even better, although it did sound as though he was just now being condescending. That's another word they don't use.

"What is this? A xylophone?" I ask, walking closer.

"A *marimba*," he says firmly.

I stop in my tracks. You would think I'd just called it a warthog. "Well, I'm sorry," I say, getting a little mad. "What's the difference?"

"A marimba is larger and has resonators. These brass tubes that hang down below the bars are the resonators," he says, pointing. The tubes have different lengths, the same way the bars do. "The tubes give the notes a fuller tone." He takes one of the rubber-tipped mallets and strikes one of the reddish brown wood bars. It makes a nice round note that lingers a while after he lifts the mallet away.

"Does this belong to the music department?"

"No, it's Robert's."

"Robert who?"

"Robert Wormer."

"But . . ." I stop. Why is he talking about Robert Wormer like he's another person? "Uh. How did you get interested in playing it?"

43

"Robert's parents inherited it from a great-aunt a couple of years ago. His mother kept it in the corner of their living room as a kind of interesting decoration. Then she decided he should learn to play it. She thought it would be kind of unique to have a kid who played a marimba."

"You're kidding!" I say, remembering my mother's same reasoning with the cello lessons.

"Are those the only two words you know? 'Great' and 'kidding'?"

I get mad again. "No. I also know 'evoke' and 'condescending.' "

That takes him by surprise and he doesn't say anything for a few seconds. Then he smiles. It's the first time I've ever seen him smile, and it's wonderful.

"Well, good. Good," he says. "You want to try it out?"

At first I don't know what he's talking about, then he holds out one of his mallets to me. I take it warily and come around to stand next to him. The marimba has two sets of bars arranged like the keyboard of an organ, with one set of bars up higher and behind a first set. I tonk the mallet down on one lower bar. Then a higher one. "I don't know what I'm doing," I say.

"That's okay. It's how I started."

I hit a few more, but it's like the cello all over again. Except without Mr. Graveston. "What are the bars made of?"

"Rosewood."

"Here, you take it back. I'm just not musical. Could you play something else?"

"How about 'Chopsticks'?"

"You're kidding." And then I slap my hand over my mouth. Only this time he seems not to notice.

He concentrates, his forehead wrinkling up, his eyebrows dipping toward his nose and then arching up and out like the wings of an angry bird. Oh no! Not birds again.

He begins. Sure enough, it's "Chopsticks," but it's not like any "Chopsticks" I've ever heard before. After the usual beginning, Robert just takes off. The music builds as though it's trying to go somewhere, trying to break out of the room. I can't believe how beautiful it sounds swirling all around my head. And then it's gone and Robert puts down his sticks.

"Wow, Robert," I say, careful not to add the phrase "that was great."

"Peter."

"What?"

"Peter Lavoris."

I look at him for a couple of seconds. Here is this guy with wonderful eyes and smile, who just lifted me off my feet with the music from an instrument I've never even heard of before, but he keeps talking as though Robert Wormer is off in another room.

" 'Lavoris' is a mouthwash," I say calmly.

"Naturally. The family fortune was founded on my grandfather's formula for it." He puts his mallets and music away in a little briefcase and walks around the marimba over to me.

"Then why does Mrs. Cronski call you Robert Wormer?"

"Because in her class I am Robert Wormer. In music class I'm Peter Lavoris."

45

"I thought you said you were Charles."

"No. She just asked what I'd like to be called. And I told her."

I might as well be dealing with the Chinese language again, except instead of being in my math book this time it's coming out of the mouth of this person in front of me. "You can't just change names when you feel like it," I say.

"I don't *change* them, I *am* them. There's a difference." He starts to walk around me.

"But you also said you were a bird," I call after him.

"Only in the social studies hallway," he responds, going out the door.

Then he's gone. There's a good possibility that I've been dreaming all this. But when I look around I see the marimba still standing there. First I think that if this is what it takes to get to know a boy then I'm not going to live very long. I'll get such bad headaches that the crack in my brain will widen until my whole body just splits down the middle. Then I think that maybe all guys aren't like this. Look at Jimmy Pinto. Jimmy Pinto would never act like this, he's predictable.

But that doesn't make him attractive. In fact, there probably aren't *any* guys like Robert Wormer. And, strange as it may seem, I like that.

I rush out of the room and look down the hall. "Hey!" I yell. "Who are you right now?"

"Harold," he says without turning around. "Just call me Harold." And he disappears around the corner.

Harold leaves me with a lot to think about. Only I don't like the name Harold. If he has to be anything at all I'd rather call him Peter. But he's only Peter in the music room. Except on Tuesdays and Thursdays the music room is locked up. Does that mean he's somebody else on Tuesdays and Thursdays? He must make out a chart to keep it all straight! I wonder if he's ever an Irving? That would be terrible. Irving would be a name to have in detention. Or Percy. He would be a Percy if he belonged to the Chess Club. Who is he when he sleeps? Does he have a different name in his dreams? What about when he wakes up and looks in the mirror in the morning? Does his reflection have a name all its own?

To make matters simple for myself I'll just call him Robert in my head. He can be whatever he wants to be outside, but inside he'll stay Robert.

As the week passes, every time I run into Robert he stops and introduces himself to me, then goes on. The names he gives always vary. Sometimes they just sound funny, like Rupert Fishpoker or Gerald Streetpillow.

Other times they belong to historical figures. Once he was Thomas Jefferson, Benjamin Franklin, and George Washington all in the same day — I think he was in a Colonial mood. Often I have to go scrambling to the library to look people up because I've never heard of them — Mrs. Cronski keeps running into me there and thinks I'm working on a special project. Only rarely is he something other than a person. Except for being a bird that one time, the only other animal he has become is a snail. He's taking track and I think he was trying to get out of gym class one day.

It's all great fun.

And I stop missing Van quite as much. Although I do get reminded of her on Friday.

On my way to my last class of the day, something on the hallway wall catches my eye. When I go up to read it I see that Van's speech plans are proceeding. It says:

!VANDELLE BARNSDORF PRESENTS!
A MONOLOGUE ON WOMEN
THEIR ROLES, THEIR GOALS AND DREAMS
THURSDAY, MARCH 6
AUDITORIUM
ADMISSION FREE!

In the margins are Xeroxed pictures of women like Amelia Earhart, Susan B. Anthony, Margaret Sanger, and Joan of Arc. I kind of think that last line shows she might be a little worried about attendance. I don't know if saying it's free will be enough, though. The organizers of our class elections last time had to put out doughnuts and soda to make sure kids would come out and vote.

When I go into the English hallway for my class I pass another poster on the wall, only this one has been ripped in half. A little farther down I see Jimmy Pinto standing in front of another. He's inked out letters in Van's name and is now putting mustaches on all the women's pictures. I've never tangled with Jimmy by myself before, and even though Van's not my friend anymore I feel I should do something.

"What are you doing, *Pinto Bean?*" I know Van said you can't fight fire with fire, but it's the first thing I can think of. At least it gets his attention. As usual, he's ready with an intelligent reply.

"What?"

"I said what are you doing? How would you like it if somebody messed up your poster?"

"I'd smash their face in. Is that what you're going to do?"

He's got me there. And now that he's not bent over scribbling on the poster anymore I'm reminded how tall he is. "No. Fighting is never an answer."

That is the wrong thing to say. For Jimmy fighting is the only answer. "Look," he says, jerking his thumb at the poster, "I believe in men and women being equal. I don't care if you're a girl. Doesn't bother me a bit. Go ahead and take a swing at me, I'll defend myself. You just better be ready to defend *yourself*."

I can see by his eyes that he really wants to hit me, and my face starts to hurt right where I expect his first punch to land. I'm not a speaker like Van, with a big vocabulary and a good idea of how to put words together, and I'm not artistic like her. I can't color my hair in that just perfect puke green, and I can't draw well enough to paint an eye on my tongue when I need one. I can't do anything. I'm just dumb Lisa, who's in a bad spot and is going to look like Frankenstein after the doctor stitches her face back together.

Then I get an idea. I don't really know where it comes from, it just appears. I open up my eyes as wide as I can and say, "I am The Black Death."

"Hunh? What are you talking about? Just make a couple of fists and try to take a poke at me."

"Haven't you ever heard of The Plague?"

"Who?"

"The Plague."

"Sure. He's a professional wrestler on TV. Fights sometimes with Hulk Hogan."

"No-o-o-o," I say in this deep, windy voice that comes out of my mouth without my even thinking about it. "It's a disease. It killed one tenth of the people in Europe once. You die in a-a-a-agony, with your neck swollen up and your face turning bl-a-a-ack. Hold still. Just one touch from me and you'll get it, Jimmy Pinto. Just one touch, and then it begins." I raise my hand like a shriveled-up claw and reach for his shoulder.

"What are you talking about? They let you in school sick? Hey! Get away from me." He backs up, looking at my face for signs of bubonic plague, probably wondering why my parents didn't keep me home in bed.

"What's up, Jimmy?" One of his friends appears.

"She's got something, Pete. Don't let her touch you. She's got something *nasty*." Then he disappears into the crowd, and I slip into my room just as the bell rings.

After school I'm dying to tell someone about it, and for the first time it isn't Van I'm thinking of. I hang out by the line of buses, and when I see Robert I run up to him.

"Hi."

"Hi," he says, and stops.

"I was The Black Death today. In the English hallway."

Robert looks at me, puzzled for a couple of moments, then the smile I saw in the music room returns. "I see."

"Jimmy Pinto was almost my first victim," I say proudly.

"Good choice."

"I thought so. The only problem was that he might have gone down in the history books. You know, as the only person to die of something from the fourteenth century."

"It might have been his only accomplishment in life. You should have given him the chance."

"Oh well." We stand there smiling at each other, and all of a sudden we're friends. I can feel it. Just like that.

The buses start to move off. He turns to watch them rumble out of the circular drive. "Uh-oh. Looks like I'm walking today."

"I'm sorry I made you miss the bus."

"Well, it looks like you missed yours, too."

"No, I walk to school. Where do you live?"

"Over by Northrop Elementary. It's a little bit of a hike. But not too bad."

I'm glad he's not mad about my making him miss the bus. But I'm still a little upset about it, being the first day of being friends and everything. So I say something I've never said to a boy before in my life. "You have to go right by my house to get there. You want to stop by? Have something to eat?" I bite my lip.

"Sounds good to me, Lisa," he says, still smiling.

"Doris."

"Who?"

"I'm Doris right now. And you?"

"Fred. Fred Dopplemyer." And he holds out his hand.

"Doris Crookshank. Pleased to meet you." And I shake his hand.

On the way to my house Robert starts telling me about himself. Or maybe it's Fred who's telling me about Robert.

51

Anyway, he says, "He got tired of being Robert all the time. It's kind of a dull name, don't you think? Not much pep to it."

"Lisa's not the best name to have in the world either," I say, although I haven't really thought about it.

"Well, one day Robert was going to school and this man stopped in his car to ask for directions. He gave them to him and the man said, 'Thanks, uh . . .' And Robert said, without thinking, 'Dave. Dave Waring.' So the man said, 'Thanks, Dave.' It took Robert a while to figure out why he did it. Then he pictured this guy in his head, clean-cut, Eagle Scout, always on time for school and ready to help little old ladies across the road. *That* was Dave Waring. That's the kind of name for a guy who gives out directions to people."

"Not Robert Wormer?" I ask.

Robert hesitates. "Maybe. Once upon a time."

"But not anymore? How come?" I ask, really kind of curious.

"Look, forget Robert Wormer. Let's concentrate on Fred Dopplemyer. He's a guy who . . ."

"Who misses buses." I jump in.

"Right. Who misses buses. In fact, he's never on time for anything. He wears glasses. There's always at least one shoelace untied, and he keeps having to tuck his shirt back in."

We both laugh. Then I think about it. "That sounds a lot like my dad." I look at him. And we both laugh again.

"That's okay. Fred's a basically nice guy. I mean, I wouldn't *be* him if I didn't like him at heart. Now what about Doris Crookshank?"

I think a minute. "She's kind of a problem kid. She wears glasses, too. And dresses that are about ten years out of style. She keeps to herself most of the time. Sits in the back of classes. She doesn't have too many friends . . ." and then I trail off. I've been describing myself, except for the glasses and dress, of course.

"Yeah? And?" he says, waiting for me to go on.

"This is my house," I'm able to say, glad to have an excuse to quit talking about Doris.

Inside, Cody is on the living room floor with all this stuff I've never seen before — coloring books, strange colored blocks, and things I don't recognize.

"This is my brother, Cody," I say. I'm always a little apprehensive when strangers meet Cody. I can always tell when they're smiling on the outside and feeling sorry for him on the inside. I'm almost sorry I talked Robert into coming.

Robert squats in front of Cody, reaches out and puts a hand on him. Then he looks at me and says, "No."

"No?"

"No. 'Cody' is not dynamic enough for him. This . . . this is a special kid. He's been around a lot for a kid his age. He's seen stuff we haven't, I bet. What do you think?"

How could he know? That's the first thing I think of. How could he know about Cody just by looking at him a few seconds, touching him? "In real life," I say softly, "he's an astronaut. This is Commander Coatrack."

Robert looks surprised. Then he turns to Cody. "An honor, sir. I've heard a lot about your space explorations, and it would be an unexpected privilege for me to shake your hand."

53

"Ahh," says Cody, and smiles when Robert shakes his hand.

"Hello, Lisa," says my mom, coming into the room. "Who do we have here?"

I didn't expect my mom to be here today, only the sitter, and it takes me a few seconds to recover. Meantime, Robert straightens up from the floor.

"Mom, this is . . ."

Robert interrupts, holding out his hand. "Elvis," he says, "Elvis Presley."

✦5✦

Mom raises an eyebrow. It floats to the top of her forehead and locks into place. "*The* Elvis Presley?" she asks.

"That's right."

Mom looks at me. My mouth drops open, but all she gets from that is to see my tongue lying in there as if it's fainted dead away. She looks back at Robert. "I thought you were . . ."

"Dead?" says Robert. "Just a trick so that I could quietly retire. All the attention from fans was getting too much for me."

Mom looks at me again, but my tongue is still unconscious. "You look a lot younger than I would expect," says Mom. Her other eyebrow decides to join the first.

"An excellent job by a plastic surgeon," says Robert. "My plan to retire wouldn't have worked if I still looked the same. I wouldn't have been able to go out in public."

"I see. I see," says Mom. "So now that you have all this time to yourself, what do you do with it?"

"I go to school. I'm in the same grade as your daughter, Doris."

Mom's eyebrows, which had started to sink back into place, now rush back up, so high they almost get lost behind her bangs. This time she looks at me and doesn't stop looking. "Doris? Lisa, have you two gotten into a school play?"

My tongue finally springs to life before Robert can say another thing. "Not exactly, Mom. He missed the bus and is on his way home. I told him he could have a snack before he walks the rest of the way."

Mom looks back at Robert, who is smiling. "Well." That's all she says. I think she's in shock or something. It's not every day that her daughter brings home a dead rock star.

I nudge Robert and he follows me to the kitchen.

"Give Cody something too, will you?" calls my mom.

"Okay," I tell her. I turn to Robert. "What's wrong with you?"

"Nothing's wrong with me." He looks real surprised that I sound mad.

"Look, at school that kind of stuff is okay. But not around my mom. Not around *grownups*."

"I did it in front of Mr. Hummel and you didn't seem to mind."

"You also quit it when he was going to take you to see Mr. Mann."

Robert waves me off. "Your mom was getting into it. She was asking me these great questions and I had to come up with the answers."

"But what's wrong with your real name? Aren't you ever Robert Wormer?"

He frowns and sits at the kitchen table. He's got something to say, but he keeps his mouth shut tight. Just then Cody wanders in, looking to get refueled. He comes over to Robert and stares into his face. Then he opens his mouth like a baby bird that wants to be fed.

Robert smiles. "Well, Commander. Back after a long mission, hunh? Kind of tired of all that space food you have to squeeze out of tubes?" Cody keeps standing there, expecting Robert to drop in a bug.

"Here, give him a cracker. He loves them." I hand Robert a sleeve of wheat crackers and go back to fixing something for ourselves. Out of the corner of my eye I see Robert give him a cracker. Cody starts making his trash compactor noise while grinding it up.

"Is the Commander here part android? He seems to have a unique system for eating."

I turn around in time to see Cody spit the cracker into his hand, put it back into his mouth, chew a while more, and spit it into his hand again. "*Cody.*"

He doesn't pay any attention to me. After all, he *is* the Commander.

"You can't do anything about it. You can't yell at him, he just doesn't understand. Once he gets into one of these moods you have to let him go ahead with what he's doing," I say.

"Oh, I don't know about that. Seems to me his programming just needs a little dusting out. A few adjustments." When the cracker makes another grand entrance into his mouth, Robert takes two pencils from his pocket and puts one in each of Cody's hands.

"Now, as Wolfgang von Otterbein, master electronics and robotics engineer, I will fine-tune the Commander's delicate instrumentation. Please hold on to these sterilized tools, Commander. If you drop them I'll have to put them back in the Micro-Detoxifier for another eighteen hours. Now, let's see." Robert reaches out and tweaks Cody's ear. Then he pushes in his nose like a button. Finally he places the fingertips of both hands on top of Cody's head and starts dancing them around the way he would on a keyboard.

Cody just keeps chewing and chewing, his eyes roaming all around after Robert's hands.

"Ah, I think we're on to something here." Robert takes another pencil from his pocket, places the eraser against Cody's forehead, and starts turning it like a screwdriver. He does the same thing to one cheek, then the other. In the meantime, Cody has his hands full and he swallows his cracker. He opens his mouth for another and Robert feeds him, then goes right back to fiddling with the pencil. After a while, Cody's full, and Robert declares the Commander fit for duty.

"Aw-w-w-w," says Cody, with a big smile.

"You're welcome, sir," says Robert, taking back his pencils. But then Cody starts to whimper. "Oh, I understand," says Robert. "You may need these to make minor repairs yourself. By all means, you must keep them." And Cody, happy as a clam, ambles out of the kitchen with his two prizes.

"I can't believe it," I say, bringing us each a sandwich. "How did you know to do that?"

"Simple. It's exactly what Professor Otterbein would have done."

Well, Robert may sure be weird, but I have to admire him for the way he handled Cody. I've never seen anything like it before in my life. And I've never seen Cody take to somebody the way he did to Robert. I'm surprised at how easily I can open up just because of that.

He's a good listener, too. I talk a long time about school, then tell him what my parents do. He doesn't believe me about my father until I open up the pantry and show him a zillion jars of free samples.

"That explains my sandwich," he says, looking at the double-thick layers of peanut butter slapped between two slices of bread.

He still won't talk about himself. But through Professor Otterbein I do find out that Robert and his family have just moved from Oklahoma, but Oklahoma is not where he's from originally. His father's in the air force and they've been stationed all over the country, and he doesn't really know how long they'll be here.

The phone rings. Mom hollers that it's for me and I pick it up. It's Van.

"I just thought I'd see how you were doing," she says. My heart leaps. She's going to give me another chance!

Oh no.

I look over at Robert. What am I doing? How can I tell her that, yes, I've changed my mind and I do believe all boys are scum, when he's sitting right there?

She's waiting.

"I'm fine," I manage to say, sounding as though I've just gotten back from a trip to Acapulco.

"Have you seen my posters?"

"Yeah. I caught Jimmy Pinto messing with one. I told him to knock it off and he left." Which isn't *exactly* true, but it sure sounds good. When I say that I can feel Van getting mad.

"I should have known it was him! Where did you see him?"

"In the English hallway."

"Well he must have done one in the home ec. hallway too. You know what he did? He cut out pictures of naked women, chopped off their heads, and attached one beneath each portrait on my poster. Susan B. Anthony looked like Marilyn Monroe! It was ruined, so I just took it down. I almost got killed in the process."

"How come?"

"Well, I only noticed it because of all the boys crammed in around it. And when I tried to take it down they started a riot. Now do you see why I have to put myself on stage?"

"I admit they can act pretty rotten," I say tentatively, glancing at Robert. I just can't help adding, "But you can't hate them all just because of a few."

"A few! I only got that poster taken down because Mr. Mann showed up and chased everyone away. But he wouldn't let me have it. No, he said he was going to take it to his office to use as evidence in case whoever did it was caught. I'll bet. He just wants to keep it in his drawer so that he can take an occasional peek at it."

I'm sunk. Why did I have to make him miss the bus? Why did he have to act so nice to Cody? And to me? Lying would be so much easier if I'd never brought him here. But

I *have* to defend him now. "Well, I'm sorry. I still don't think you should put them all in one group."

There's a long pause at the other end of the line. Then Van says, "It's *him* you're talking about, isn't it?"

I bite my lip. "Him and others," I say, without sounding very convincing.

"Oh no, no others," says Van, with an edge to her voice. "Just him. Bringing you over into their camp. Next thing you know, you'll be fetching his slippers and lighting his pipe. Well, I was going to ask you to help me make up some new posters, but just forget it. I'll get Marcia to help me."

"Marcia? Marcia who?"

"Marcia Tyler."

I almost break out laughing. Marcia Tyler is one of the most popular girls in school, with boys dripping off her. So how could Van get her to help? It can't be true. "Oh yeah?" I say.

"You don't believe me, hunh? Well, just for your information she helped me get out the first batch of posters. She's a strong believer in what I'm trying to do."

"What about all those boyfriends she's got?" I ask.

"She's giving them up."

"She's what?"

"You heard me."

"Now I *know* you're lying," I say.

"You can believe as you like," says Van, unconcerned. "But she *is* going to be helping me. And while we do it, over at her house, we'll probably watch television. *Lots* of television."

That does it. She's just stuck a knife in my stomach and

twisted it around. I'm so upset I can't think straight, and my voice gets caught trying to yell at her. I happen to look at Robert, who's stopped chewing on his sandwich and is staring straight at me. I can't believe she's doing this, getting me so worked up that I can feel the tears filling the corners of my eyes.

Then it all goes away.

As though I was born with it, this quiet, serene voice comes out of my mouth and goes into the phone. "Why . . . why, sugar, you ain't got no call to be tellin' little ol' lies to me."

There's another pause, then Van explodes, "What are you doing?"

"Why, whatev-vah do you-all mean?"

"Lisa! Are you mockin' me?" Van's own accent kicks in as she heats up.

"No, ma'am. Jest tryin' to talk to you-all, one gal to anotha'."

"As who?"

"Jest call me Scarlett."

Have you ever seen a movie called *Gone with the Wind*? Well, there's a lady in there called Scarlett O'Hara. I don't know where she came from, but all of a sudden she's in my head and talking out of my mouth.

"He's done it!" screams Van. "He's brainwashed you! He's got you acting just like him! Well, if you gave in that easily, then, frankly, my dear . . . you can go to *hell*." And then she hangs up.

I put up the phone feeling kind of dizzy. I've never really tangled with Van before, I've always been too unsure of myself. I didn't think I was smart enough, for one thing, and for the other I've always gotten tongue-tied. Like just now, after she threw all that stuff about watching television at me. Like with Jimmy Pinto this afternoon. Like with the kids who tease me about my grades. If somebody intimidates me, I usually freeze up. But both times today I saved myself, instead of just standing there silent, wondering what in the world to say. I turn with a smile on my face to Robert.

"That was pretty good," he says.

I sit down. "Having another person around to do the talking is pretty handy."

"It's always worked for Robert," he says.

"I don't know how I've gotten along this far without it. Thanks."

"What for?"

"I got the idea from you."

He laughs. "That's the crazy part. *Anybody* can do it. It's not that hard. If you're sad, you just become somebody who's happy. If you're scared, you become somebody who's brave. In fact, if everybody did it the world would be a lot more peaceful."

"You can say that again." I just wish that for a minute Van could become *anybody* else, just to see another point of view. No, not just anybody else. I wish she could be me. Then she'd know how much I still like her, despite all the dumb things she said. I stop feeling dizzy and start feeling sad.

Robert points to the phone. "Who was that?"

"Vandelle Barnsdorf."

"No, I mean really."

"Vandelle Barnsdorf. Van. She's in our history class. Sits at the back of the room on top of her desk?"

"Oh, *her*. What a great name. She's really wild looking. And you're friends with her? How about introducing me next time?"

I almost choke on what's left of my sandwich when he says that. "I don't know. We're not getting along too well these days."

"Is that why you became Scarlett O'Hara?" he asks. I nod. "Good choice. I was once Rhett Butler, myself."

"You were? When?"

"At my last school there was this girl who wouldn't leave me alone. She kept trying to get me to hang out with her." My heart gets a sinking feeling when I realize that girls at our school might be interested in doing the same thing. "So I finally told her, 'Frankly, my dear . . .'"

"Yeah, I know how it goes. Van just gave me a new and improved version."

"Oh."

I twist a corner of the tablecloth, not sure if I want to ask him this next question. "Who do you become if somebody says they don't like you anymore? Somebody who was your friend for a long time?"

While Robert thinks, I start squirming around in my chair as though I have to go to the bathroom. I must look like a worm on a hook. What's worse, I *do* have to go to the bathroom.

Finally he shrugs. "I wouldn't be anybody," he says. "I'd be the bird. I feel best when I'm a bird. I feel free. I don't have to worry about people problems anymore."

I stop squirming and look at him.

"But then Robert's never lived anyplace long enough to have a friend like Van. So, I don't really know who you should be."

"Never?" I ask. He shakes his head. "Gee." Somehow never having had a long-time friend seems worse than losing a long-time friend.

"Maybe," he says, "you could keep on being Scarlett."

"Do you-all think so?"

"I shorely do, Miz Scarlett."

"You-all know? I think you-all may be right. I think I'd feel even betta with a mint julep in my hand."

"I could use one, too, Miz Scarlett."

I get two glasses of water out of the tap and plunk in some ice cubes. On second thought, I put two plastic flowers from my mother's bud vase in the glasses.

"Ah-h-h," says Robert, smacking his lips, "mixed to perfection. But, I really must go, Miz Scarlett."

"Must you-all?" I ask, fluttering my lashes.

"Yes. Frankly, my dear, I've got to do some homework."

We both get up and turn and find my mother standing in the doorway with this really weird expression on her face.

"Ma'am," says Robert, tipping an imaginary hat to her as he goes past. I smile weakly and follow him to the door. When I come back my mom is sitting down at the kitchen table.

"*Who* was that boy?" she asks.

I sigh. "His name is Robert Wormer."

"And *what* were you doing?"

"Just kidding around."

Then she starts teasing me in a way I really hate, pretending she's seriously confused about everything. "Does he often become Elvis Presley?"

"No, just in our living room."

"I guess I should feel privileged, then." She pats her heart.

"Oh, Mom."

"And who was he in the kitchen, then?"

I mumble something.

"What's that?"

"Rhett Butler."

"That makes sense. How does he like our plantation?"

"Oh, Mom."

She gets this sly smile on her face that I know means trouble. "Is he your boyfriend?"

"Mother!" I yell, and stamp my foot.

Cody starts to cry in the other room.

"See that," says Mom, "you've made him think I'm beating you." She goes into the living room and I follow. Cody is so happy to see me without any bruises that he climbs up into my lap.

"Can you act civilized?" she asks me.

"Just don't get personal." Cody sticks a pencil in my ear, trying to adjust my programming to Mom's liking.

"Listen, I am the person who washes your underwear. If that's not personal then I don't know what is. So I think I'm entitled to a *little* information."

"I can go back to washing my own underwear," I say, "just like I used to."

Mom sighs. "Honey, I'm just interested in you, okay? This is the first person you've ever brought home since Van.

The first boy. I think that's wonderful. Boys are a pretty important ingredient in a thirteen-year-old girl's life, I think."

"Not to Van," I mutter.

"Does Van still not like boys? Is that what your fight with her is about?"

I don't say anything.

"Okay. Too personal. Back to Robert." I fill her in on where he's from and what his father does and all that. I also tell her that he plays the marimba. I try to tell her what it sounds like, but she just sits there and smiles. I guess she had to be there. When I'm through she says, "There, that wasn't so bad, was it?"

I shrug. "Now I feel like you took something away."

"What do you mean?"

"Well, Robert is brand new. I don't think he has many other friends yet. I don't know. I just wanted to see how things went before you met him. Now that you know about him it might jinx things."

"Lisa, you sound superstitious. What were you going to do? Keep him a secret?"

"Yeah," I say.

"Oh." Mom sits there thinking. "Do you really, really like this boy?"

"I don't *know*, Mom."

"Okay. Okay. No more questions. How about taking that out before you hurt yourself?" She points to the side of my head.

Cody's on the floor now, having left the pencil stuck in my ear. Can you imagine? I didn't even know it. How can you argue seriously with your mom when you've got a pencil hanging out of your ear?

I finally remember to ask her something I meant to ask when I first got home. "What are you doing here? Where's Mrs. Jameson?"

Mrs. Jameson is an elderly woman who takes care of Cody during the day. Cody's gone through a number of sitters. He used to wipe out about one every six months. Mrs. Jameson has been with us the longest. I think it's because she's almost deaf and Cody can't get her attention.

"I've adjusted my schedule with the agency," says Mom. "I have to pick up Cody from school and bring him home."

"Oh yeah. I forgot. How was your first day, Commander?"

"Aw-w-w-w."

"Liked it, hunh?" I ask Mom.

"He seemed to. And we've been going over his homework."

"Homework?" I look again at all the stuff laid out on the floor that I saw when I came in.

"Well, not real homework. You see, he needs reinforcement for what he does in school every day or else he'll forget it. I can't do the physical therapy, of course, but I go over with him what he and all the other children went through today with the teacher."

"You mean, like have the same math class twice in one day? Gee, Cody, and I thought *I* had it rough."

"Well, it's an overview. The teacher tells me what needs to be stressed."

"Can I help?"

My mom looks sort of embarrassed when I ask. "Well, I kind of want to do it on my own. For a little while at least."

So I leave them alone and go on up to my room. I putter around for a little bit, feeling kind of lost. Then I realize it's because Cody isn't up there puttering around with me the way he usually does in the afternoons. I sit down on my bed, not quite sure what to do. Then I get back up. I lift my arms out to the side and look at myself in the mirror.

"I am . . . a bird."

✦6✦

Robert says that the only thing to do now, since I showed him such warm hospitality, is to repay me with an invitation to his house.

When he tells me this he is Sir Walter Raleigh.

I almost tell him no, because of Cody. Then I remember that Mom works with him in the afternoons now. So, after school I phone my mom and she says it's okay, and that she'll pick me up before dinnertime. She sounds real happy for me, but she doesn't say anything dumb and embarrassing.

Riding Robert's bus is kind of strange. I don't recognize any of the kids. Robert and I sit in the back away from everybody and he starts pointing out features of interest like a tour guide in Hollywood. By the time we reach his house he's pointed out the Dairy Queen, named after a woman of royalty who abdicated and came over here to raise cows, the cemetery, where all the graves secretly empty into a big warehouse from which the bodies are shipped off to the government for horrible experiments, and the Big Lanes bowling alley, home to some pins that are actually aliens from another planet — after closing they beat up on the bowling balls that have been running over them all day.

We're laughing pretty hard by the time we get off the bus. Things change after we get into his house.

Robert's house is like mine except that it has pictures of planes, jets, or helicopters covering every inch of the walls. There's a military uniform in a dry cleaning bag lying over the back of a chair, and on the mantel is a picture of Colonel Wormer himself, looking into the sky kind of startled, like a jumbo jet is coming in to land on his head or something.

Mrs. Colonel Wormer comes downstairs when she hears us, a little surprised to see me just as my mom was to see Robert, only she looks more disappointed than happy. "Why, Robert, who's your little friend?"

I look down at myself. Nobody's called me "little friend" since I was five years old. I figure it must be because I'm still pretty flat-chested. Nobody seemed to notice much when I hung around Van, they were too busy staring at her to notice that I didn't have much up top.

But I figure she must be okay to have a neat son like Robert, so I decide to do what he did yesterday. When he says, "Mom, this is . . ." I jump in with, "Annie Oakley."

But instead of smiling or even looking surprised, she says sternly to me, "Now *stop* that." I almost get her wagging finger in my eyeball. Then she turns to Robert. "I would appreciate a little seriousness."

I sit stiffly on the sofa. Robert drags himself over beside me.

"Now, we're all comfortable," she says, trying to fasten

the skirt button at her waist when it's already buttoned. It's one of those skirts that has buttons running from your ankles to your belly button. It must take her fifteen minutes to get into. My dad hates them. My mom had one once a few years ago and my dad — he was in his goosing mood that day — came up to her and asked what if she needed to get it off in an emergency. He didn't know I was in the room at the time, and I asked what kind of emergency. He looked at me for a while and then said, "What if it caught fire?" At the time it made sense.

Well, Mrs. Wormer takes a deep breath and finally seems to relax. She says politely, "Could you tell me your name, please?"

"Lisa Archer."

"Thank you."

I look at Robert. "You're welcome."

"It's nice to finally meet one of Robert's classmates," she says, still real polite. "Would you two like to play a board game? Monopoly?"

I'm still looking at Robert. I can't believe he's brought me here to be trapped by his boring mom. He finally stands and says, "We just want to talk a while. I thought I'd show her my room." That sounds like a great idea to me. Anything to get away from that deadly finger of hers.

Mrs. Wormer says, "Robert, it's not *polite* to take a young lady to a boy's room."

Robert drops back onto the sofa as though he's been shot. His hand starts crawling uncertainly up his chest, searching for the bullet hole.

"We can talk right here," she says. "You can start without me while I fix something to eat. Are milk and cookies all right, Lisa?" I nod my head, but she keeps standing there. Finally I think to say "Thank you," and her smile comes back and she goes out to the kitchen.

As soon as she leaves I open my mouth, but Robert stops me. "I am Sitting Bull, you are Crazy Horse, and *she*" — pointing to the kitchen — "is Custer." I'm not sure I'm in the mood for this right now, but I don't have time to argue. Custer comes in with a silver tray loaded with cookies and three glasses of milk. Yes, she's going to have cookies and milk right along with us.

"Robert?" She holds out a glass for him to take.

"Ugh," says Robert.

"I *beg* your pardon?"

"Thank you," Robert says glumly. It seems to me that the Indians are going to get beat this time around.

After that she asks me all about the classes I'm in and how long I've lived here and who my parents are. She sounds pretty much like my mom. She ignores Robert until she's given me the third degree, then she says, "You have a nice little friend here, Robert," and gets up and leaves the room.

"Come on," says Robert, and I follow him into their backyard.

After we walk in silence for a while, I say, "I guess you can't be Sir Walter Raleigh when you're at home, hunh?" I liked that one. When he asked me to his house today he picked up my hand and kissed the back of it. It was almost the most wonderful thing anybody's ever done. But he surprised me so much I yanked my hand away and it smacked him in the nose.

"Sure I can," he says with a slight smile. "Sometimes

it's just not worth the trouble, though," and he jerks his thumb back toward the house.

I turn around and see Mrs. Wormer looking at us from an upstairs window.

"Most of the time it's just better to shut up. Robert's used to that. Especially around his dad. Robert tends not to argue with him." He grunts. "Neither does Robert's mom. See, that's why I think Van is so great."

"You do?"

"Sure. Robert ought to send his mom to hear her speech. Believe it or not, if Robert's dad told her not to, his mom wouldn't vote. She agrees with him on everything. Including how Robert should be raised."

He sits down and starts pulling up his backyard. Soon the air smells of onion grass.

"You know how you get to be a colonel? By always being right. But if Robert's dad is always right, then Robert tends to always be wrong. If he comes up with an idea on how to fix his bike, and it's not the way his dad would do it, even though Robert's way works, then it's wrong. Because of that Robert isn't allowed to grow up to be like anyone else but his dad. And if Robert doesn't want to grow up to be his dad, well, that's tough. That's wrong. That's . . . being a nobody. Robert the Nobody. Robert the Nonexistent."

Robert suddenly jumps to his feet and throws out his arms. "But Christopher Columbus exists! Or he did. And you can't say that the way *he* did things was wrong." Robert acquires an Italian accent.

"I tink I wheel sail . . ." He wets a finger and holds it up to the wind. His eyes light up. "Dat way," he finishes, and points. "West. And discover lots of land where rock stars can flourish."

I laugh. "He didn't say *that*."

"How do you know? After all, he figured out the world wasn't flat. Who's to say he didn't see Michael Jackson in his dreams, break-dancing on the yardarm of the *Pinta?*"

Robert makes a disastrous attempt to break-dance and ends up in a heap on the ground. When we both quit laughing, I lean over to him, still puzzled.

"What about school? How come Robert can't be Robert there?"

"Ahhh." He waves my suggestion away. "Teachers. Kids. Parents. They're all the same. They all expect you to act a certain way. Teachers want you to show up on time, be quiet, and do homework. Kids want you to wear the right clothes, talk cool, and snub kids that are in cliques other than their own. No, Robert can't be himself there either."

"How do you know I'm not one of those kids?" I ask.

He sits up and gazes into my eyes. "Because you are Queen Isabella." He says it so quietly and seriously that a chill runs down my spine.

"I am?" I say, just as quietly.

"Yeah," he says in his normal voice. "So could you lend me a few bucks to cruise to America?"

"*You.*" I swing at him and miss. He grabs my arm and we end up tugging and grabbing at each other and generally laughing like idiots.

At the front door the most sickening exchange takes place

between our two moms. It goes something like this:

"So nice to have met you, Mrs. Wormer."

"The pleasure was mine. You have such a charming daughter."

"Why, thank you. We enjoyed having Robert over for a visit yesterday."

"Well, it seems like they're going to be great friends, and I hope we'll see more of her."

"I'm sure she'd like that."

"And we'll have you and your husband over for dinner sometime just as soon as we can."

"That sounds lovely. We're in the phone book, and if you'd like to reach me during the day just call Westover Realty and leave a message."

"Wonderful. Good-bye."

"Good-bye, now."

During this whole thing I can see Robert standing behind his mother holding his throat and rolling up his eyes. I have to bite my lip to keep from laughing.

When we get in the car my mom says, "Well! Robert seems to have a very nice mother."

"Hunh," I say.

"Just think, if you and Robert hadn't become friends I might never have met her."

"Don't blame that on me," I say.

Mom glances away from the road to look at me. "What are you talking about?"

I tell her everything Robert told me about his parents, trying very hard to make her see Mrs. Wormer's true side. But as soon as I finish my mom says, "That's just terrible. I feel sorry for his parents."

76

"Sorry for his *parents*," I say. "What about sorry for poor Robert?"

"Well, I'm sorry for him, too, but I'm more sorry for them. I think it's awful to have a child who runs around telling stories like that."

"Stories!"

"Lisa, I'm sure Robert is upset about something, or else he wouldn't have said all those things. But I doubt his parents are the unfeeling ogres he makes them out to be."

"But she's just a phony! She only acts nice because you are another adult!"

"Lower your voice, Lisa. I'll have to roll down the window just to let out all the noise you're making." She makes a face at me and I slump back in my seat. "I think it's lucky that he has a friend like you, now, to help him with his feelings. But I think you'd better try to be objective about his family life. His parents have their point of view too, you know."

I don't say anything. I'm too mad. I can't believe Mom is letting me down. I thought maybe I could get her and Dad to talk to the Wormers and try to straighten them out. But now I see that's hopeless.

"Where are we going?" I ask when we zip by our street.

"We have to pick up Cody. I'm sorry, I forgot about him staying later today, or I would have been able to let you play with Robert longer."

Play? I start to wonder if she wasn't with Mrs. Wormer a little too long. "I'm not six years old anymore, Mom."

"Let's see. You were born on . . . right, and then Cody . . . Yep, you're right. You're just about twenty-seven, **aren't you?**"

"Very funny."

"What's gotten into you?"

"Skip it."

We get to the hospital and park. Mom leads me to the pediatrics section, and at the end of the hall we go into a room. It looks just like a schoolroom for little kids. The walls are decorated with all the usual pictures of moms and dads with their faces finger-painted into place. There are shelves with books and magazines, there's a corner with toys piled in it. The only difference is, there's more than one teacher, and the kids aren't all the same age.

"They group all the children by ability rather than age," Mom says.

There are screens set up so that a teacher can close off a section of the room to herself and the kids she's working with, and when the teachers want everybody together, to sing or something, the screens can be pushed against a wall.

"There's Cody over there," says Mom.

He's sitting over near the toy section with another little kid. The kid has on real thick glasses and a back brace and he's playing with a block that has four wheels and a pair of handles on it, rolling it forward and back between his legs. Cody is behind him with his arms wrapped around the kid's stomach, his eyes closed and his head leaned against his back. It looks as though they're on a motorcycle, with Cody just along for the ride.

"Looks like you've found a buddy," I say. At the sound of my voice Cody opens his eyes.

"Ah-h-h!" he says, seeing me and Mom. He throws up his arms to us, and for the first time we realize that the other kid was depending on Cody's arms to hold him up. He goes toppling over, crashing onto the floor. I've always said motorcycles are unsafe.

"Oops. What happened, Martin?"

A nice-looking woman comes over to us and kneels by the kid. Martin is still on his side, trying to figure out why he wiped out. The woman sets him upright. "That brace is so awkward for him sometimes," she says. Martin goes back to his race, pushing and pulling the block.

"Mrs. Jenkins, I'd like you to met my daughter, Lisa. This is Cody's teacher." We say hi.

Mrs. Jenkins looks down at Cody. "Who is this you've been playing with, Cody?"

"Ma-a-a," says Cody. "Ma-a-a-a."

"That's right, Ma-ar-tin."

She's getting him to *talk*? My eyeballs almost fall out of my head, which Mrs. Jenkins notices.

"Yes, we're working on a few words, aren't we?" She picks Cody up and he reaches a hand for her throat, just as I've wanted to do with a few of my teachers. But instead of strangling her he just feels the vibrations as she repeats, "Ma-ar-tin. Ma-ar-tin." And she puts ...and on his throat to feel his response when he tries to imitate.

"Hey, Mom," I say. I turn to her and see her eyes starting to fill up like goldfish bowls. "What's wrong?"

"Talking. He's talking," she says. "We should be thankful for Dr. Barnes."

Dr. Barnes. Immediately I start scowling. I forgot that he put Cody here. Big deal, so Cody can make a few extra noises. So what? It's just another way of screwing up things and getting my parents' hopes high for nothing.

We collect Cody and his stuff and get in the car. On the

way home I say skeptically, "How come Cody hasn't tried to talk to us before?"

"Maybe he has, and we just didn't know it. Maybe we just didn't pay attention." She wipes at her eyes. "Anyway, because it's so difficult for him he probably just gave up. Settled on the sounds he could make and just stuck with those. Developed his own language."

"His own language?"

"Sure. You know what certain sounds of his mean, don't you? Like when he pretends to have a gun. He makes the same sound every time, doesn't he? He makes an association and it stays in his memory. That's what language is all about, isn't it? And that's what learning is all about."

I look at Cody wedged between us on the front seat. He doesn't look any different, but Mom is making him out to be this other person. Has the real Cody been hiding out inside while I've been playing all these years with the Cody on the outside? The thought is spooky and I start to get scared. But just then he looks up and smiles at me, and I know she's wrong. He is, and always will be, the same wonderful little kid.

At home Mom and Cody work at making more dumb noises. Cody keeps one hand on Mom's throat and the other on his own throat. For a long time they work on "u," and after about five minutes of "Oooooo, oooooo, ooooo," I start to go nuts. They sound like a pair of cows waiting to get milked. I ask if I can help with dinner, but Mom says that since it's Dad's turn tonight I'll have to wait and ask him when he gets home.

Upstairs, I read an article about this high school that

wants to send a pregnant rat up in the space shuttle to see how it would react to giving birth in weightlessness. Can you imagine being the poor rat and watching your babies float away as soon as they pop out? How would you feed them, with two on the floor, three on the ceiling, and one twirling around right in front of your nose like a ballet dancer? NASA has their request under consideration.

When I hear Dad come home I wait until I know he's gotten comfortable and is ready to start rummaging around in the kitchen, then I go down.

"Hi, Dad."

"Hello, L.A., Lisa Archer."

"Need any help?"

"Still no confidence in me, hunh?" He stands up with a pan from under the sink and tucks his shirt back in. When he pulls out his hand his shirt tails come with it.

"Dad, you know I like the way you cook. Can't I just chop something up for you?"

He drops the pan and picks it back up. "No, no, everything's under control. You just go ahead and have fun. Do whatever it is teenagers do these days before they eat dinner."

"They usually get hungry."

"Fine, fine, you just go ahead." He's staring into a cookbook that Mom got him as a Christmas present. The book is not for gourmets. In fact, none of the recipes have more than three ingredients in them. There's also a line in the introduction about always getting a grownup to light the oven for you.

I sit down at the table just in case he changes his mind

and notice a glass jar sitting there. It's got what looks like seeds inside. "What's in the jar?"

"Wheat. Bad wheat."

"What's wrong with it?"

"It grows about six inches tall, and dies."

"How come?"

He stops looking at the cookbook and turns to me with a sigh. "I wish I knew. It's a hybrid, a combination of different types of wheat. We've been working on it for a long time. We thought we had all the right qualities finally packed into each one of those little seeds. To grow tall, stand tough, be loaded with grain, and ripen quickly." He shrugs. "But it grows six inches, and dies. Something got in there that we didn't want. Or maybe there are too many good ingredients, too many for the plant to handle at the same time and still grow properly. I don't know." At the mention of ingredients he goes back to looking at the book.

"Are you sad?"

He smiles a little. "Yeah. I guess so. It was a pretty big project."

I go over and put my arms around him. "I'm sure you did everything you thought was right."

He puts a hand on my head. "Yeah. But sometimes, Lisa . . . sometimes that isn't enough." He looks over at the jar of wheat.

"Where did I put the Crisco?"

✦7✦

To get my mind off Van I practice being other people when I'm at school. But I can't tell if I'm very good at it because I don't try to talk to anybody. It's kind of hard to be a convincing Pocahontas when nobody knows who I am but me. Only once do I ever say anything out loud. I tell a cafeteria worker, after they run out of Jell-O for dessert, "Let them eat cake" — I'm Marie Antoinette at the time — but she gives me a plate of cookies instead and waves me on.

Robert keeps bugging me about meeting Van. I finally do introduce them, but it's only by accident. We run across her coming out of a rest room at lunchtime, wiping a damp tissue across her forehead. I look closely to see if she's trying to get rid of another eye, but I don't see a thing. We're going in opposite directions, so we sort of have to stop and say something. She looks Robert up and down.

"Van Barnsdorf, I'd like you to meet —" I don't even

try to finish my sentence. I just step back and let Robert announce himself as whoever he happens to be at the moment. I also step back to get out of the way of any fists that might come flying from Van's direction.

"Robert Wormer," he says, and extends his hand.

I almost drop my books. He was Elvis to my mom, but he's just plain Robert for Vandelle. He must really want to impress her.

But he doesn't succeed. "I thought you were the birdman of Fletcher Junior High," says Van.

"Ms. Barnsdorf, today I am someone who's anxious to get to know you. Our forebears brought to this continent a new nation, conceived in liberty, and dedicated to the proposition that all people should have equal rights. Now we are engaged in a great struggle, testing whether this nation, or any nation so conceived and so dedicated can long endure. We are met on the battlefield of that struggle. And I would like to dedicate my services to you in the cause of that struggle."

He says it all so fast that it takes me a few seconds to figure out what it all means. It sounds beautiful.

"Forget it," she tells him. Then she turns to me with a little less anger and says, "You've got to be kidding." Then she walks away.

I look at Robert. "Was that really Robert Wormer?"

"Abraham Lincoln," he says. "Gettysburg Address, with a few changes."

"Well, why didn't you tell her that?"

"I needed to be Robert Wormer to show that I was sincere, but then I needed Abraham Lincoln to express my feelings eloquently.'' He looks after Van. ''Didn't do much good, did it?''

''She's just obstinate,'' I say.

''Why won't she let me help?''

I sigh. ''For one thing, you were with me, and she and I still aren't speaking. For another thing . . . she doesn't like boys.''

''Hunh? How can she expect to win equality for women if she doesn't get men over to her side?''

''Because I don't think she wants equality. She wants women to be in charge and for the men to see what it's like to be always given a hard time.''

''Oh,'' says Robert quietly. ''Must be tough on her father.''

''No, she loves her father. You see, I think basically Van's a good person. Just unreasonable sometimes.'' I shrug, not really knowing the answer.

We go into the auditorium, where eating is not allowed, to eat lunch. We hunker down near the front row and eat from our brown bags. The curtain is up and there's a work light on at the rear of the stage, a bare bulb at the top of a floor lamp, looking like a little bald man's head on a very skinny neck. When Robert gets down to his apple he jumps up on stage with it and paces around. After a while he finds an umbrella, opens it, and holds it over his head.

''I say,'' he says, with a British accent, ''wouldn't you like to get out of this nasty weather?''

I giggle and take the side stairs up to the stage. My accent is not very good. ''It's making my spot of tea rather damp,'' I reply, getting under the umbrella.

"Isn't tea supposed to be damp?"

"Yes, it works much better that way, doesn't it? But you see, the tea bags are in my pocket, and pockets are very difficult to sip from."

"Quite, quite. Have you considered keeping a teacup in your pocket? Then you'd be prepared for such an emergency."

"What a jolly good idea. Perhaps I should carry two? One in each pocket, so that when I joined a gentleman under his umbrella we could share."

"Capital, my dear! Simply capital!"

"Oh dear, I just thought of something."

"Why, what's that?"

"The rain is cold. How do we get hot tea from cold rain?"

"Ah, I see your point. Well, I could put out my cigar in it, but then we'd have the ashes wouldn't we? No, no, won't do. Don't care to have ashes in my afternoon tea. Hmmm. I've got it! We'll just have to get angry."

"Get angry?"

"Yes. Very, *very* angry. In fact boiling mad, if you get my meaning?"

"Oh! Yes! *Steaming* mad."

"Precisely. Hot under the collar!"

"So hot we'll stew about it."

"Simmer!"

"Froth at the mouth."

"Exactly. And we'll just hold on to our cups until they're nice and warm, then have a pleasant tea."

"Capital!"

"Splendid!"

"My hero!"

"At your service."

And without warning he bends down and kisses me on the mouth.

Giggles, hollers, and applause break out at the rear of the auditorium where some kids have been watching our performance. Oddly enough, I'm not embarrassed. After all, I've just been to England, met a gentleman, and received a kiss on my lips that wasn't from a relative or my father.

Van is definitely wrong about him.

"Bye, Robert," I say when we split in the hall.

"Lord Hastings," he replies.

It's a relief to get to the weekend. I feel exhausted. I'm still bothered about Van and can't figure out what to do. And Robert. I know there's such a thing as a friendship kiss. My parents are always giving those out when we have company over. But then there's the kiss that means something more. Which did Robert give me? I kind of feel that if it was for friendship, then it wasn't very special. But it's also scary to think it might have meant something more.

Fortunately, I can always come home, where I can count on things. Where I feel back in control. And this weekend I'm looking forward to a lot. For one thing I can forget about everything and everybody else. For another, I'm bound and determined to finally spend some time with Cody. Maybe it's my imagination, but it seems like every time I haven't been busy with homework or some chore around the house, Mom's been playing teacher with him. But tomorrow I'm going to get up early and whisk him away to new adventures before anybody else even opens their eyes.

On Saturday morning, though, it turns out I don't get up quite early enough. When I look out my bedroom window, I'm just in time to see Mom driving off with Cody. I rush into the basement, where Dad is replacing a frayed cord to one of our lamps.

"Where's Mom going with Cody?"

Dad looks at me. "Good morning."

"Good morning. Where's she taking Cody?"

"It's all right. She's required to bring him back. Says that in our marriage contract. Article 3, paragraph 4, 'All children that are products of this marriage must be brought home within twenty-four hours until said children reach the age of twenty-one. After that the parents/prison guards/ trainers may start renting out their rooms.' "

"Dad."

"She's taken him over to visit a friend."

"A friend? What do you mean? Since when does Cody have friends?"

"Ow!" A piece of the wire in the cord stabs Dad in the finger. He takes his hammer and whacks it three or four times, teaching it a lesson.

"Hello?"

"What? Oh. It's a friend from school. Uh, I think his name is Burns. Martin Burns."

The kid on the motorcycle. He must have survived the crash and gone on to win the race. And the prize is my brother. "When's he coming back?"

"I don't know, honey. What's the problem?" He looks at me, his wounded finger still in his mouth.

"I just feel like I haven't seen him in years."

"Years?"

"*Yes.*"

"Well, Lisa, aren't you glad Cody's got somebody to play with finally? Somebody his own age? Somebody who . . . sees the world the way he does?"

"*I* can see the world the way he does. I've been doing it all his life."

"But you're still not what he needs."

When Dad says that I feel as though he's taken the hammer and swung it into my stomach.

Dad sees my face and hurries up to say "I'm not saying he doesn't love you anymore. Lisa, you know that would never be true. I think he probably loves you more than either your mother or me." He pauses, playing with the cord. "But he's developing interests in others. It's . . . it's called socialization. It's good for him. Just like going to school. You see that, don't you?"

No, I don't. "I'd planned out the whole day for him."

"Well, now you've got it all to yourself. Do whatever you want today. It's all yours."

Great. My day was laid out as carefully as one of my grocery lists, but Mom set a match to it and now Dad wants me to play with the ashes.

Halfheartedly I ask, "Do you need any help with that?" I point to the lamp.

He looks down. "No, I think it's dead now. Should be easier to manage."

"Do you have any other chores to do?"

"Lots. But I'll get to them. You just take it easy and enjoy yourself." He smiles.

I *enjoy* myself by sitting in the living room waiting for Mom to come back. While I'm in there I look through Cody's school things on the coffee table. Among them is a big, square piece of cardboard with the alphabet on it. The letters are big and raised, so that I can run my finger over them and feel the distinct shape of each.

Then something comes to me.

What do I really know about any of these teachers that are in the school with him? They might not understand what Cody's all about. How's he getting along without me to watch over them, keep them in line, stop them from doing something that will upset him? Do they respect him the way I do? If they don't, he's going to start feeling rotten. And how can Cody get out from under that feeling when he's stuck there all day?

I think about Martin Burns. He's probably a good little kid. But how can I be sure? Maybe the back brace and glasses are a disguise. The perfect way to get out of regular school. He can sit in the hospital school all day, play, and run the lives of the other kids when the teachers aren't looking!

. I picture them at twenty-three, Cody on the back of Martin's chopped-down BMW, sitting in the parking lot of a 7-Eleven. Martin tells Cody the plan by talking to him in his rearview mirror — he can't turn around to talk because of his back brace. "You go inside, rub out the clerk with that gun I stole, then take the money. When we leave we'll take the river bridge and you can toss the gun over the railing." Cody nods. The gun looks enough like a cucumber. He gets off the bike. Then Martin topples over.

I see how dangerous it is to have Cody out of the house so

90

much. Especially at this age. Maybe when he's a little older, but not now.

I start to feel panicky. When I hear the car pull into the driveway I rush outside.

"Thanks, honey, but I've got them."

Got who? I'm looking into an empty car. When I turn around I see she's holding two bags of groceries in her arms.

"This is all I bought," she says. "Just a bit to hold us over for a while. You can shut the door for me, though."

I slam the car door. "Where is he?"

"At Martin Burns's house."

"I already know that."

"Then why did you . . . ?"

"Why didn't you bring him home?"

"Lisa, he's only been over there a few hours. Let him enjoy himself."

"What am *I* supposed to do?" She looks at me blankly. "When was the last time he ever spent a weekend away from us?" I ask.

"I know. Isn't it wonderful?" She's sounding an awful lot like Dad, making me think their brains have a satellite hookup.

I try again. "When was the last time I ever had a weekend without Cody?"

This time she gets it. "You miss him?"

"Of *course* I miss him. That's not the point. The point is that he's with strange people. Do you want him to grow up to be an ax murderer or something?"

My logic, though it is perfectly clear to me, seems to go over her head. We're standing on the front stoop and I still haven't opened the door for her. We don't move, Mom waiting for me, me waiting for Mom. To a passing motorist we probably look like one of those plastic deer statues. "Look, Martha, they've got one of those plastic mother and daughter statues." "I think one would look nice on our stoop, don't you, Herman? Let's go to the K Mart and see what they've got."

Mom looks into one of her bags, then at me. "Ax murderer?"

"Well, maybe not that bad."

"Can we discuss this inside? The ice cream is sitting next to my stomach and freezing my belly button." We go into the kitchen and put things away. Dad comes up to say hi. We look at him. He looks at our faces and turns around and goes back downstairs. "I wasn't expecting you to be so jealous of him, Lisa."

"Jealous? Wait a minute . . ."

"How else do you think you're acting? Cody as an ax murderer?"

"I said that maybe he wouldn't be that bad."

"I should think not. So just how bad do you think he *will* be? On what grounds do you think he has to grow up bad at all? Why couldn't he grow up just as badly by remaining here with us?"

"Because he'd be with me," I say firmly, "and I'd never let it happen."

Mom relents. She comes over and puts a hand on my head. "I'm sure you wouldn't. But couldn't we give Martin a chance? He's an only child. He doesn't have a sister like you to look after him. Maybe some goodness Cody's picked up from you will rub off on him."

That gets to me, right in the old heart. I never thought of Martin being helped out by Cody. It makes sense, though. I shrug at Mom.

"I know you miss him. Try to think of him as temporarily on loan."

"On loan? Like a library book?"

My mother giggles. "Well, not quite. But Martin has a few more physical problems than Cody and has to go in for an operation soon. Cody will help keep him cheerful."

Right then I feel doubly worse for thinking badly about Martin the Mad Motorcyclist. "Sure. If it'll help Martin to have Cody as a friend, then I can't complain." The problem is I still want to complain. I feel I have the cards stacked against me and that if I want Cody back again I'll have to *really* come down with the plague. I don't like being in the position of feeling sorry for somebody and yet at the same time still feeling that I'm losing out. "I guess I'm not a very magnanimous person," I say aloud.

My mom laughs. "I think you're the living, breathing definition of it."

"You're teasing."

"I'm trying to be sincere without being mushy. You want me to be mushy instead?"

"I don't know."

"Let me try, then . . ." She gets real serious. "I think you're a wonderful person, warm, full of love, generous, caring . . ."

"That's enough." I break away from the hug she starts to wrap around me.

"Well? Which do you prefer?"

"Maybe you can get Dad to pinch-hit for you."

"Thanks a lot."

By the time Cody gets back that evening I'm dying. I think I know what a chocolate candy addict goes through, because I need a Cody fix so bad that when Mom brings him through the door I tackle him and smother him in kisses. He squeals and fights me off, then pulls a picture out of his pocket.

"You made this at Martin's?"

"Ma-a-a. Ma-a-a . . ."

"Yeah, I get you." I look at it. "You paid somebody else to do this, didn't you? I know little boys like you can't *possibly* have this much talent." Cody's not sure what I'm saying, but he seems pretty happy about my reaction to his picture. I'm not sure what it's of. It looks sort of like a train crashing into the side of a giant meatball, although I have to squint real hard even to get that much.

"Okay, young man, let's get in some studies before dinner time."

I look at Mom, dumbfounded. "I just got him back, and now you're taking him away again."

"For heaven's sake, Lisa, he's not going any farther than the living room."

"But I've been waiting for him all day!"

Mom ignores me and gets out all the implements of torture that relate to Cody's schooling. "The more we go over this . . ."

"I know. Reinforcement," I say.

"Exactly."

I sit down, resigned to another hour of listening to the cows moo at each other. When she gets out the cardboard

94

with the alphabet on it, I ask, "Are you expecting Cody to read?"

"We don't know yet. Maybe someday."

I shake my head. "Why are the letters raised like that?"

"Because all children learn differently. And we not only have to find out what Cody can learn, but how he can learn."

"What do you mean?"

"Well, this alphabet, for example. The letters are raised so that he can run his fingers over them. Some children need to call on other senses, besides sight and hearing, in order to learn. Some need to touch, to feel, before meaning sinks in. Touching it may make it more real to them, more understandable. You can't label a child dumb just because he doesn't catch on like everyone else in the class. It may just be a matter of his or her approaching the same lesson or problem from a different angle, and then they might understand it just as clearly as anybody else. Do you see what I'm saying?"

I nod my head, not believing a word. "Like eating an ice cream cone," I say. "Some people lick down, then nibble away the cone to get the rest of the ice cream. Others bite off the bottom and suck out the rest. It's the same ice cream in both cones, but it just doesn't taste as good unless each kid can eat it his own way."

Mom looks at me like I'm a television with the sound turned off. Her neck is stretched out, she's got an ear cocked to me, and her eyes are peering out of their corners in my direction. "I sup-pose . . ." she says very slowly. Then she straightens up. "I guess you know what I'm talking about." Then she shakes her head, trying to free up the gears in her brain that jammed with my reasoning, and focuses on Cody.

I decide to make one last-ditch effort. "Isn't he too tired to be doing this now? It's been a long day for him."

But even as I speak, Cody crawls up on the sofa beside Mom and starts making happy sounds about all the stuff in her lap. Mom just looks over at me. "I think he wants to bite the bottom off of his cone."

✦8✦

Nothing happens all at once. In fact it seems to happen so slowly and naturally that it's as though it was always bound to be that way.

First of all, Van's speech goes off on schedule. Practically the only person in the audience, though, is Mr. Mann, checking to make sure she sticks to her word and doesn't turn any lights on. Instead she uses the work light to read by, having set it next to the podium. You see only half her face the whole time, the darkness having chopped off the other half. The speech is pretty good, except it's a little hard to follow, what with men first being oceans, then fires, then geysers — geysers since they're always fussing and shooting their mouths off.

The big shock is that Marcia Tyler really is there supporting Van, although the way I hear it she's only doing this to get back at Tony Bradford, the football team's star receiver, who dumped her a little while ago. Without Marcia there would probably be no audience at all. She talked all of her cheerleader girlfriends into showing up and they're sitting in the front row, snapping their gum and twirling their permanents the whole time.

When it's over Marcia leads the applause, which is kind of a signal for the cheerleaders to shoot out of their chairs, do splits in the air and cartwheels across the floor exactly the way they do whenever the team scores a touchdown. Van looks embarrassed. Robert and I stay in the shadows in the back, and when it's over we slip out quietly.

Another thing is that I'm still seeing very little of Cody. Martin the Mad Motorcyclist continues to be a hot item with him. They're always together on the weekends. And during the week, it seems as though he can't wait to get home and fool around with Mom. By the time they're done he's too tired to play with me. A lot of times he nods off right in the middle of a game, holding his cucumber in one hand, without ever firing a shot.

Then something suddenly comes to me. Something that's been bothering me for weeks, but that's been only a question mark in the back of my head, a question mark without any words in front.

When the words come I ask my mom, "How are you able to get such regular time off to pick Cody up and work with him in the afternoons? I thought real estate people were always running around."

Mom blushes. Mom *never* blushes, so I know I don't want to hear the answer. "Well," she begins, "I'm not actually an agent right now. I'm a part-time secretary for the agency. Like I was at your school."

"What?" I explode. I get really upset. "You left that job

to make more money. You left it to get outside, to meet more people and help them find nice homes."

"Lisa, Cody needs help and support from me right now. Your father is making a little more money these days, so we should be all right for a while." It's true. Dad's reputation as a peanut butter connoisseur has spread, and now it seems every peanut company in the world is sending him samples. We're making room in the basement.

"Why did you keep it a secret from me?"

"I just didn't want to say anything because I know you don't like me giving up on things. Like . . . like I did with Cody. Well, I'm not really giving up my real estate ambitions, they're just on hold right now."

On hold? I feel that I'm the one who's been left on hold, while everyone else shoots off in their own direction. I always have time on my hands, and there are only so many science journals I can read in one week. And my parents are still being independent, running the whole house without me, right down to pouring the milk for my corn flakes in the morning.

I start spending more time with Robert.

Getting to school now seems a relief. When I get together with Robert I can drop Lisa Archer and her problems at the front door and just become a rock star, or a movie star, or even a character out of a novel. We're a great team. A lot of times we play husband and wife, not anybody from real life, just somebody made up. Like Mr. and Mrs. Waldo Rat-scum: we'll sit at a cafeteria table with our jackets stuffed under our shirts so we look eight hundred pounds over-weight and ask each other to pass various nonexistent dishes back and forth so that we can add to our bulging bellies.

"Honey bunch, could you pass me that bucket of possum toes?"

"Are you sure you have time for a whole bucket, sugar beet? Remember, they're dividing an old plow horse in half for us as the main course in five minutes."

"Five minutes? Hmmm. Well, perhaps I'll just take the possum toes out of their skunk skin wrappers, put them in a blender, and drink them down."

"That sounds like a whomping good idea, tulip bulb."

The kids around us usually start gagging and holding their hands over their mouths when we start talking about the Ratscums' diet. There's always somebody wanting to sit down and watch, the way they did in the auditorium. We've sort of become popular. People who used to look through me now smile at the two of us in the hallway. It's kind of nice to be recognized. I still don't act outrageous on my own, though. And when I go home every day, I become Lisa Archer again.

Van, of course, is appalled by the way I'm behaving. Robert just ignores her cold stares whenever the three of us meet. He doesn't try to impress her by being Abraham Lincoln anymore. Since she stormed off that time he treats her like anybody else. "If that's the way she feels," he said once, and shrugged. It doesn't seem to bother him. The more attention he's gotten at school, the less he's been interested in expressing an opinion about the women's movement. Or about anything else.

That's another thing. I don't know how he really feels

about me. He doesn't seem to want to be with anyone else but me, male or female. And we've kissed several times since he was Lord Hastings — he says he's never Robert Wormer when he does it, but I have no doubt that they're his lips pressing against mine.

I'd like to think that since the names he comes up with are his idea that the desire to put an arm around me comes from him too. But I run into trouble every time I try to find out.

When I go over to his house for the second time I manage to work up the courage to try and clear things up. I begin by saying, "Excuse me, uh . . ."

"Professor Horace Flagellum, expert on microorganisms."

"Yeah, well, uh . . . could you leave us alone for a minute?"

"Eh?"

"I'd like to talk to Robert, alone, for just a little while."

"Robert? Robert? I don't seem to recall . . ."

"Hello-o?" I reach up a fist and knock lightly at his forehead. "Can Robert come out for a little while?"

"I must protest. This is highly irregular."

"Robert? I just want to know . . . why you kiss me. I mean, is it what you want, or is it just pretend?" It takes a real effort to get that out, and I have to look at my toes almost the entire time.

He looks at me for a moment. Then he says, "Robert has a message for you."

"What? Oh. Okay."

"He says, 'Tell her I'm taking a shower right now and will get back to her as soon as I can.' "

"*Robert*. Please?"

"Let me try again," says Professor Flagellum. He clears his throat. "Now, see here, Robert, this young lady deserves a proper answer. Put it in zoological terms if you must, but give her an answer." He looks at me. "He's thinking."

"Uh-hunh."

"Ah, here he comes. Yes, I see." He looks at me gravely. "He wants me to pass along the following: 'I do not get involved with women. Not in a romantic sense. It is too scary.' "

In a way I feel relieved. After all, I'm only thirteen. Having a boyfriend seems like an awful big step right now.

Then he says, "I must say that this young man's message does not show much spirit. Do you see him often?"

"Actually, hardly ever, Professor."

"Well, that's probably for the best. He doesn't seem very mature. If he was an amoeba I doubt he'd even know how to divide. But, be that as it may, it's good news to my ears. Because it means you are free and unattached for gentlemen like me who come along." And he bends down and lays a big one right across my mouth.

See what I mean about being confused?

I just try not to think about it though. I'm having a great time, otherwise. I don't think I've ever laughed as much in my life as I do when I'm with Robert. It's nice.

One day we run into Jimmy Pinto. I've heard that ever since the bird episode Jimmy has gone nuts trying to figure Robert out. Every time the two of them meet Jimmy tries to find some way to tick Robert off, but Robert always manages to remain calm and leave Jimmy speechless. Which, considering Jimmy's vocabulary, is probably not hard to do. I haven't seen Jimmy since the bubonic plague became my #1 most admired disease. I wonder now, though, if I'm coming down with the real thing, because at the sight of him my stomach has suddenly started churning.

He stops in front of Robert and me and considers, trying to remember, maybe, if he's supposed to be somewhere else. Off making somebody give up their lunch money or causing a microscope to disappear from the biology lab. Finally, he decides he can spare the time. The first thing he says is directed at me. "You ain't sick."

I would laugh if I wasn't so scared. Jimmy's not by himself this time, and, with loads of muscle standing just past his shoulder waiting to be called into action, I start looking for escape routes or teachers. Robert brings back my attention.

"What is your name, please?" he asks Jimmy.

"I'm not listening to nothing. Not from you. Not from her. It's time to show us your feathers, birdbrain."

"Jim Pinto, is it? Well, Jim, I'll tell you what we're going to do." Robert reaches for his wallet and pulls out a five-dollar bill. Jimmy's mean smile immediately disappears and is replaced by the sort of expression people get when they're hypnotized: vacant and unblinking.

"Now, Jim, I'll *give* you this five-dollar bill if you can . . . show me your history homework for today." That's a safe bet. Jimmy never does his homework.

"What are you doing?" asks Jimmy, still semidazed by the money floating before his face.

"Jim, I will give you this five dollars, free and clear, if you have your homework on you. No strings attached. Free and clear . . . for your homework. Do you have it?"

"No, I don't ca-"

"Then I'll give you another chance. Do you have . . . an acorn in your pocket? If you picked up an acorn on your way to school today, this five dollars will be yours."

Jimmy digs into his pockets so hard you'd think he was a regular back-to-nature type of guy who's always collecting leaves or molted feathers. "That's a stupid thing. I don't . . ."

"Tell you what," says Robert. "I'll make it even easier. If you've got a penny dated 1940, the money is yours."

That *really* gets Jimmy scrambling. He frantically turns all his pockets inside out, then snarls at his friends to do the same. He goes through the change littering the palm of his hand, turning over pennies. It's actually quite a treat for me, seeing that Jimmy can actually read. I'm trying very hard to keep a straight face. Kids are starting to gather around, always up for another Robert Wormer performance.

"Find that penny . . . find that penny," Robert softly encourages him. "Find that penny and win the money . . . or *trade that money for what's in my assistant's pocket*."

Jimmy's head snaps up. His eyes fly to my pants pockets and try to turn on their X-ray vision.

Taking my cue, I jam a hand into my right front pocket and start wiggling it around.

"What's in there?" Jimmy asks quietly, a bead of drool just starting out of the corner of his mouth. "What do I get? What's . . . ?"

"The penny first, Jim. Find that penny," Robert directs him. I keep playing with one crumpled Kleenex and my house key.

"You guys?" asks Jimmy, turning around. None of his buddies has the right penny either. He turns back to Robert. "What else? What else can I have? There's *got* to be something easier than *that* to look for."

Just then the second bell sounds. The hallways quickly empty.

"Sorry, Jim," says Robert. "We're out of time. But listen, you come back, and next week that money may be yours. Thanks a lot. So long." Robert actually shakes his hand before moving off. I don't dare look back, but I can hear Jimmy swearing at his friends and instructing them to carry acorns with them from now on.

As we walk on I ask, "Monty Hall? *Let's Make a Deal?*"
Robert smiles and nods.

By the time I reach history I've daydreamed through most of the rest of my classes, thinking about Robert. He is somebody special, and I'm awfully lucky to be hanging around with him. He's got the school in the palm of his hand, and as long as I can keep watching him, maybe I'll learn to work up the confidence he has. It seems so simple. All he has to do is . . .

"Lisa Archer, are you listening to the question?"

It's then I notice that Mrs. Cronski is looking straight at me. I also notice that I have no idea what she's talking about. "Lisa, please stand."

I get up, a little shaky. This is her method of punishment. Stand you up so everyone can get a good look at what a dope you are.

"Lisa, would you like to repeat what I just asked?" she says, knowing I don't have the slightest idea.

My face turns red. That's the horrible thing about faces, if you have fair skin they always give you away, no matter how casually you stand or how firm your voice sounds. You don't get a chance to fool anybody. I figure that right now it looks as though my cheeks have been hit with a double helping of tomato sauce, hold the meatballs. I hate it, I really do. And there's nothing for it but to stand there until Mrs. Cronski decides I've had enough of the titters and giggles from the rest of the class and lets me sit down. I want to get out of looking stupid so bad I could scream.

I think that's when my brain shifts without my really thinking about it. All of a sudden I'm by myself, facing down Jimmy Pinto again. We've been studying American politics during World War II, and this voice, sounding pretty close to mine, says, "Do you know to whom you are speaking?"

"What did you say?" says Mrs. Cronski.

All I need to see is that startled look on her face and I'm off and running. "Eleanor Roosevelt has no need to answer silly history questions. I *am* history. A living, breathing cornerstone of my era. Perhaps I should be asking questions of *you*. Tell me, have you heard of my husband, Franklin?"

You could hear a pin drop on a ball of cotton in that room. I've stunned them all, and I can *feel* that. I have control of the classroom all of a sudden. I've just yanked it away from Mrs. Cronski with a couple of words. I'm the stronger one, the same way I was that day with Jimmy. Mrs. Cronski is the student now, and she has to sit and learn the lesson from me.

106

Mrs. Cronski says, carefully, "Yes. Yes, I have heard of your husband. How is he doing these days?"

"Quite well, thank you, considering the war and all."

The class follows us like a tennis match, swinging their heads to watch my replies bounce off Mrs. Cronski and hers fly over the net to carom off me.

"Tell me," she says, "what do you think your husband's greatest accomplishments have been?"

She's sent me a forehand smash and I have to think about my readings from last night before I can answer. "I think when he urged through his proposal that the federal government take over our commercial and economic system in order to get us out of the Depression, and then had politicians accept his programs for giving people work, were among his better moments."

"And the name of this set of programs? I can't seem to recall it."

A soft lob that I handle easily. "The New Deal."

"Ah, yes. And perhaps you could mention some of your own achievements?"

I can't believe it. Mrs. Cronski is actually playing along with this. Robert is a genius. I flash him a glance and note a big grin on his face directed toward me. "Well, I served as a delegate to the United Nations, and I was chairwoman of the U.N. Commission on Human Rights. But probably my most satisfying year was 1948, when I led the way in writing the Universal Declaration of Human Rights."

She asks me more questions but never manages to trip me up. I'm usually pretty good in history anyway.

Finally she says, "Thank you very much, Mrs. Roosevelt. May I call you Eleanor?"

"Please do."

"Well, Eleanor, you've been most enlightening. That will be all."

My own grin starts to fade from my face. I'm being dismissed. I suddenly get it, and it's like having somebody crash cymbals in front of my face to wake me from a deep sleep, only in reality it's just the bell going off, ending the period.

Mrs. Cronski hasn't been going along with me. She's been using me. Going over the material from our book. Our conversation was just reinforcement, like what Mom thinks she does with Cody. She took control of the class back from me without my even seeing it. Maybe they even think now that she set up this whole thing. Mrs. Cronski has won the match with a little tap over the net.

As everyone is leaving, buzzing about what happened, Mrs. Cronski calls me up front. I don't exactly expect her to thank me for helping her cover the assignment, but I'm not ready for what she does say. Words I've never heard spoken to me before.

"Lisa, I want you to go straight to the principal's office."

◆9◆

Since I've never been here before I'm completely terrified and extremely curious at the same time. I check out the room, seeing what type of place a principal lives in. I'm actually in a waiting area. There are four squared-off chairs with cushioned seats and backs gathered around a round table. There's a bench along the wall near the door in case there's a busy day. The table is full of magazines on contemporary education that have never been opened and one *Reader's Digest* with the cover torn off. It's been handled so much that it's swelled to three times its normal size, as though somebody let it sit overnight in a bucket of water. There's one hanging spider plant over by an empty bookcase that doesn't resemble a spider so much as a dead octopus, with its long yellow tentacles hanging straight down, following the shape of the pot.

Not surprisingly, the secretary in the outer office says Mr. Mann can't see me. That's why most teachers have pretty much given up on sending kids here. But she says

Mr. Ott, the assistant principal, will be free shortly and that I should wait. That information is not comforting, because Mr. Ott usually only deals with the hardcore cases. I can tell that he's busy, because I can hear the thwack of his oak paddle against the seat of somebody's pants. Since it's not happening to me I can't tell how hard he hits, but it definitely *sounds* painful. Some guys stole his old paddle and slowly fed it into a fire out in the nearby woods last Christmas. This new one is supposedly bigger and heavier, and, in memory I guess, Mr. Ott has affectionately named it Yule Log.

Mr. Ott opens his office door to beckon me in, and my back straightens so fast I can hear it crack. As I get to his door, out comes Jimmy Pinto. He glares at me but doesn't say anything. I wondered why he wasn't in Mrs. Cronski's class.

Mr. Ott tells me to sit. There's only one other chair in his office besides his and it's a skinny metal one standing in front of his desk. We both sit down and he looks at me with his hands folded.

"You are . . . ?" he asks.

He doesn't even know who I am. That makes me feel about two inches tall. "Lisa Archer."

"And what did you do in Mrs. Cronski's class, exactly?"

I decide to stick to the plain, simple truth and get it over with. "I was Eleanor Roosevelt." It never occurs to me that maybe that isn't enough.

He stares at me for a few seconds, then says, "Excuse me?" very loudly. Then, "I asked what happened with Mrs. Cronski!" just as loud, as though he's decided I'm deaf and didn't hear the question correctly.

"I'm Eleanor Roosevelt!" I scream, accidentally, so afraid that he'll shout at me again.

This time his voice is more normal. "I thought you said it was . . . Archer. Bo Archer."

"*Lisa* Archer."

"Well what . . . ?" His eyes narrow. "No fun and games in here, young lady. How would you like me to take that down off the wall? It's all warmed up," he says, pointing to good old Yule.

They're not allowed to paddle girls here and he seems to be kidding, but my lower lip starts to tremble anyway.

"I thought so," he says. "I used to have a pretty fair batting average when I was in school. Having a bat in your hand regularly sort of gets in your blood. I can always use the practice." He cocks his right arm and pulls it slowly through the air. "What do you think about that?"

At this point the rest of my face joins in with my lower lip, like a shirt flapping on a clothesline.

"Now we're getting somewhere," says Mr. Ott.

He sits back in his chair and makes a steeple out of his two hands. He looks longingly at his white drop ceiling, as though he wants to remove a panel and go crawling around up there. But it turns out that's not what's on his mind at all. "You've heard of life throwing you curves, haven't you, Lisa?"

I nod my head, as much as I can without making my face fly completely off.

"Well, the curve used to be my favorite pitch. I had an eye for it. The only home runs I ever made were on curve balls. You see what I'm saying?"

I don't dare not nod my head again.

111

"Good. Now, it's entirely possible that a pitcher could throw a grapefruit or an orange. Even a zucchini, although I doubt it would reach the plate."

At this point my face more or less locks in midflap. I'm no longer scared anymore. That's because I'm too busy trying to concentrate on what he's saying, which seems to me not to make a bit of sense. So my face has just stopped, as though somebody swirled a spoon in it and then tossed it in the freezer.

"But the baseball is made for the bat, specifically. That's why any problem that comes your way shouldn't be regarded as something strange or exotic, like an orange or a zucchini. It's simply what it is. A problem. It can be dealt with. Just take a swing at it. So, when life throws you a curve, don't take it out on a teacher. That's a surefire way to strike out. Keep your eye on it, follow through, and you may connect. Now, this is your first time, so I'm not going to throw you out of the game."

He smiles, and it takes me a couple of seconds before I realize he means he's not going to suspend me. That frees up my face again.

"I'm going to leave the . . ." A knock comes on the door.

Mr. Ott leaves the office, but returns in a couple of seconds. "I started to say that I'm leaving any punishment to your parents. They've been informed of your behavior and I'm sure won't have any problem seeing how grave an infraction you've committed. Now. You may leave. Your mother is waiting to take you home."

*

Mr. Ott may not have done much of anything but scare me, but it was still enough. No way am I going to pretend with Robert in school again, not anywhere or any time if it's going to make me act like a dope and get me in trouble with teachers and principals. Good grades are important, they're about all I have going for me. I can't afford to mess up. What do you want to bet that Sally Ride never became Eleanor Roosevelt in front of her history teacher? NASA will probably hold that against me.

Mom doesn't say anything until we're in the car and moving. Then she starts with, "They said you talked back to your teacher. Was Mrs. Cronski a bad girl today?"

It makes me mad that Mom is always sarcastic at the worst possible times. I'm also mad because no matter how I try to explain it, what I did will sound intentional. She'll just never understand. I almost cry, but with the shape my face is in from Mr. Ott's office it seems my brain can't find the connections to my tear ducts anymore. "I wasn't paying attention . . . and when she called on me I couldn't answer. She made me stand up."

"So?"

"It was embarrassing."

"I imagine that's the point."

"Yeah, well . . . I don't know what happened. All of a sudden I was Eleanor Roosevelt. I didn't even think about it. I didn't really talk back. Well, maybe I did. I don't know."

"Eleanor Roosevelt?" She gets to a stoplight and looks over at me. "Robert."

"It wasn't his fault. He didn't encourage me."

"You can't tell me he didn't have some influence."

113

"Maybe, but not directly. You're not going to let me see him anymore, right?"

"That wouldn't serve any purpose, would it? You'd still run into him in school. And since the problem seems to be tied up with him, you'll have to work it out with him."

I look at her, surprised. "What do you mean?"

"You said what you did was an accident?"

"Yes."

"So, you don't plan on being another major figure from history in front of Mrs. Cronski again?"

"No."

"Well, if it was an accident to begin with, and you don't want to have another one, then you're going to have to take steps to prevent another from happening. Which seems to me to involve talking with Robert. I'm not going to give you an easy excuse by forbidding you to see him. You'll have to make it clear that it's your own decision, your own responsibility, to not act with him anymore."

How did she know? How did she know I was hoping she wouldn't let me see him anymore just so I wouldn't have to try and explain to him? Making A's doesn't mean anything to Robert, he won't understand my caving in to Mr. Ott. And I'm afraid. Afraid of having him laugh at me for that. I don't think I could stand it. Especially if he becomes someone like Santa Claus to do the laughing. How would you like to be mocked by Jolly Old St. Nick? It would be worse than any of the teasing I've ever gotten from other kids at school. Laughter hurts much more when it comes from a friend. And right now I'm kind of short on those.

Nothing is going right. I feel like Cinderella. All of a sudden I have to give up the good times and go back to rags and a pumpkin. And I have to tell the prince not to get anywhere near me with that glass slipper again.

"It's easier to pretend sometimes," I say, more to myself than to Mom. "I got used to it with Cody."

"But you're talking about *games*. This happened in school. Real life. There's a big difference."

Sometimes there doesn't seem to be that much of a difference, though, I think. The way Mr. Ott treats his paddle as nothing more than a baseball bat, or the way Mr. Mann hides from students. And they're supposed to be in charge of things.

When we get home, we wait for Dad before anything else is said.

Mom fills him in when he comes home and we have a family conference, another way to keep together the family "unit" — I wonder why we have to make such a big production out of everyday decisions. Cody is there as well, sitting next to Mom with his fingers jammed into his stupid school stuff, which just reminds me again about Dr. Barnes.

Dad is kind of nervous. It's been so long since we've had to discipline you, Lisa, I'm not sure how anymore."

Mom smiles encouragement at him. I sigh. I just want to get it over with.

Dad chuckles, still nervous. "Let's see, what would I do if I were Dr. Barnes?"

That does it. "Why can't you two think for yourselves?" I ask. "Why do you have to go running to Dr. Barnes every time?"

Dad looks upset.

115

"Dr. Barnes has kept us together," Mom says calmly. "He's the one factor that's . . ."

"What about me?" I say. "Who took care of Cody when you weren't around? Who helped keep the house clean? Who worked at . . . everything? I did a little of everything!" The tears missing before finally find the right doors. I wipe them away fiercely so they don't get the wrong idea. "I'm not feeling sorry for myself. I'm not trying to get out of being punished. I just want to know why he's more important."

Dad starts looking worse. He stands up and fidgets around. He has his shoes off and one sock is trying to snake its way off his foot. "Lisa, I'm sorry, we've never . . ."

"I don't think this is the time to talk about that. We're here to discuss what went on in school today," interrupts Mom.

"But I don't think she's ever understood how bad we feel for making her worry about us as well as Cody. How sorry we are. How lucky we are to have her." Dad looks at me. "To have you." Then he turns away.

I don't know what to say. I'm all mixed up, but still mostly mad.

"All right," says Mom. "Then I'll add this. And, Lisa, I'm not saying it to be mean. But do you think, by yourself, you could have brought us back to Cody? Made us understand what we were doing to ourselves and to him? And to you?" Cody starts to fuss, not understanding why everyone's so upset.

"No," I say, although I hate to admit it. I don't care if she thinks she didn't say it to be mean, she still makes it sound as though I didn't do much of anything that whole time.

"Then we'll drop Dr. Barnes and get back to you, okay?" Mom has one hand going up and down Cody's back, trying to soothe him while she's talking to me.

"I still think . . ." Dad starts again.

"You're going to make yourself sick, just like you've done in the past," Mom warns him. "It won't do a bit of good to go on and on about it."

Dad nods. "All right. All right."

He sits down, pulling his sock back over his white foot. Nobody says anything. Finally, he takes a deep breath and forces a smile. "Mom seems to think you won't do this again. At least not in a history class."

"Not anywhere in school," I say.

"Good, then. I don't really understand what you were up to . . . You want to talk about it?" I shake my head. "If that's the case, what we're left with is the simple matter of finding a punishment to fit the crime. I don't feel the crime itself was too severe, so I think we can be pretty lenient." Dad's eyes check out Mom and come back to me. "In fact, I think you can make up for it in a couple of minutes. Mom, what do you think of having Lisa give Mrs. Cronski a call to apologize?"

I should have expected it, but I'd been thinking more along the lines of being grounded and put to work around the house, which really wouldn't have been much of a punishment at all. I was looking forward to it even. But the thought of calling Mrs. Cronski makes me forget everything else for the moment.

117

Just the suggestion that Mrs. Cronski might *exist* outside of school as an actual person comes as a kind of shock. I never considered the possibility before. Who would? It's like having a nightmare creature walk out of your closet in the middle of the afternoon and say, "Hello, I've decided to become real for you today." I guess I always had some vague idea that when the teachers drove away at the end of sixth period there was some special road they all took that led to a base, like an army base, where they were kept for the night out of the way of the rest of the world. After all, I've never seen one in a restaurant, or a grocery store, or sitting in church. They just disappear until they're needed again, don't they?

But I guess not. Because here I am opening the phone book and, sure enough, there's a listing for Cronski. I press the right buttons. Slowly. Very slowly. So slowly that a recording comes on telling me I'm taking too long to complete my call. After that I whip out the numbers, not wanting the phone company mad at me too.

"Hello?"

"Hello. Mrs. Cronski?"

"This is *Mr*. Cronski."

I forgot. She's not married to Douglas MacArthur. "May I speak to Mrs. Cronski, please?"

"Moment." The phone at their end sounds like it bounces off three or four chairs and then hits the floor. The voice comes back on. "Sorry."

I hear his footsteps go into a deep dark tunnel, then faraway voices, then another set of footsteps comes out of the tunnel. "Hello?"

"Mrs. Cronski? This is Lisa Archer." I launch into this

118

apology without trying to explain why I did it, which I don't think I can do anyway. But before I get too far she breaks in on me.

"Lisa, I'm *so* glad you called." And after that it's all her talking.

You'd think I was a long-lost relative or something by the way she starts telling me her whole life story practically, about how ever since she started teaching she's wished for a student to just pick up the phone and chat. Oh, she's had kids call after they've graduated, but this is different. And isn't this wonderful that we can talk just like we're any two women getting together on the phone for polite conversation.

I don't remind her that I'm only on the phone because I mouthed off in class.

I discover, though, that she hasn't forgotten. "I realize that thirteen is a difficult age," she says, "and that things happen that you don't really mean to happen. And you're such a *good* student, Lisa. I almost hated to send you to Mr. Mann but, well, I really didn't know what else to do."

"That's all right," I say. "I didn't see Mr. Mann, though."

I hear her sigh. "I was afraid of that. So it was Mr. Ott, then. Did he give you the Super Bowl talk?"

Super Bowl talk?

"He did talk about when he played baseball," I say.

"Ah, the World Series talk. I think I like that one better anyway. He always gives one or the other to first offenders. Oh well."

She doesn't say anything else, and I get this funny feeling.

"Hello? Mrs. Cronski?"

119

She hung up. Just like that. Teachers are sure weird.

"Was Mrs. Cronski a good sport about it?" asks my Dad as I head up to my room.

"Yeah," I say. "She was all right."

A good sport. I picture Mrs. Cronski winding up on the mound, pitching to Mr. Ott — who gets a big zucchini curve ball right in the face.

I stay awake in my bed as long as I can that night, but I finally fall asleep, and the next day comes to get me right on time just like I knew it would.

I avoid Robert, trying to figure out exactly what to say to him. But by doing that, I eventually run right into Van.

"You didn't get in trouble?" she asks. She's surprised, I suppose, that I still have both my arms and legs.

"A little. I'm not getting the electric chair or anything," I answer, looking for a way past her.

"I knew something would happen. He made a fool out of you."

"I did it to myself," I say.

"You sure did. I couldn't believe it. How degrading to be tricked like that. I thought you were smarter."

Everybody is making me mad lately. Maybe some of it's left over from yesterday, but all of a sudden I'm tired of putting up with the stupid things Van sometimes says. "Van, he didn't start hanging around with me because he hates me, because he wanted to get me in trouble. And if you think that's true then you're crazy."

"He's a male, isn't he?"

"So is your father. So is my father. So is Cody. You like Cody, don't you? Or have you forgotten that?"

She knows if she says anything against Cody she'll be eating my math book, so she keeps quiet for a couple of seconds. "They don't count," she finally says.

"Why not?"

"Because they're accidents. They were supposed to be born as women, but something went wrong and they came out men."

"Hunh?"

"It happens. It's biologically feasible. They got all the feminine genes, but the chromosomes got mixed up and they came out men."

"Van, you *are* crazy."

But I get this weird picture in my head of my parents' wedding day, where instead of wearing a tuxedo, my dad's got on a wedding dress like my mom's, and they get confused when the minister says, "You may now kiss the bride," because they don't know which of them he's talking to.

I shake my head to snap out of it. "You just made that up because you didn't know what else to say."

"I did not."

"Well, then, isn't it just possible there are more men like that?"

"No. Because it's rare. It only happens once in a while in Georgia, and occasionally up here."

I slap a hand to my forehead. There's no arguing with her. Then I get a nasty idea. "Well, then, if it can happen to men, it can happen to women too, can't it?"

That startles her. But she says, "Maybe."

"Then why couldn't *you* be a *man* in a *woman's* body, hunh?"

"No!"

"Why couldn't you? You dress like one. What other girls treat their hair like you do? And what about the way you act? You want to dominate men just the way they've dominated women in the past. Is that something a typical woman would want to do? Aren't you acting just like a man?"

"No! No!" shouts Van.

Her face has turned red and she's crying. I've never seen her cry before and it's a little scary. Somehow you just don't expect to see someone with green hair cry.

"No," she says again, tearing at her earlobes, "because a man wouldn't have to lug around big fat ugly tits!"

Then she whirls away, leaving me there with a little pile of paper clips at my feet.

At home Mom is fiddling with Cody again but I don't care. When she starts getting dinner ready I have to talk to her. "Mom, do you think Van worries about her weight?"

"Honey, you know she does."

That's a new one on me. I didn't know that I knew. "But she doesn't *seem* to care. She's always the first one to *attract* attention to herself by wearing clothes different from everybody else."

"Don't you think she wears those clothes so people will look at them and not at her?" Since Mom's peeling onions, Niagara Falls has been rerouted through her eyeballs.

"How can they not see her?" I ask.

"Well, they do see her but they're more aware of the clothes than of Van. When you think of a cowboy, what do you picture in your mind?"

I think. "Ten-gallon hat. Bandanna around the neck. Checked shirt. Jeans and boots."

"Okay. Now. Couldn't a man walk through our front door right this minute in a business suit and say he was a cowboy?"

Great timing. Dad walks in the front door — "Hi, everybody, I'm home" — suit on, one shirt tail out. I giggle.

Mom smiles. "Okay. Good example. Couldn't Dad be a cowboy?"

"No."

"Why not?"

"Because he's not."

"What if he were wearing all those clothes you say a cowboy should wear. Would that make him a cowboy?"

"No. I don't get this."

"What if somebody, some stranger, saw Dad dressed like that. Would they think he was a cowboy?"

"I don't know. I guess so."

"See. They're making a judgment by what he wears. They're looking at the clothes, not at Dad. When Van wears torn clothes and chicken bones through her ears" — they were turkey bones, and she put them in after Thanksgiving — "the kids see a tough punk rocker, right?"

"Yeah. So?"

"How would she look in a dress? A plain, brown dress with her hair its natural color and permed?"

I don't say it, but I sure do think it. Van would look like any fat, teenage girl. A homely girl.

I feel a little sick inside. "But she really *is* tough. She's always been able to handle herself."

"I don't question that," says Mom.

"Well, then, why should she care what her body looks like?"

"Everybody wants to be liked. Attractive to people. I don't care who they are. Van's no exception." Now Mom has out this smelly fish. Her eyes are really getting a workout.

"Not Van," I persist. "She doesn't need to be liked by anybody."

"Oh, I think she does. Especially since you told me how she acts toward Robert."

"Why? What about Robert?"

"I think Van's jealous."

"Jealous!" I sputter. "Van hates boys. And she really hates Robert."

"I don't think she really hates boys," says Mom softly, "and I don't mean that she's jealous of you. I mean she's jealous of Robert."

"Jealous of Robert? That doesn't make any sense."

Mom looks at me, her face red and completely wet. But there's not a tear in her voice. "She's jealous of Robert because he's gotten to spend lots of time with you, and she hasn't."

I stare at her. "You think Van misses me?"

Mom nods, little drops falling from her chin and pattering to the floor.

Van misses me? *She* misses *me?*

Cody comes to stand in front of me with his mouth wide open. Automatically I feed him a cracker and he hands me a pencil.

·10·

I hang around outside the music room before school, listening to Robert's marimba. The comedians are galloping again, slamming into each other, trying to find the end of the music so they can rest and put on a few bandages. I don't want it to stop, though. I don't know what's going to happen after it does.

I saw Van in the hallway earlier. She was wearing a big sweater — probably her dad's — over her punk clothes. The sweater was so big — her dad was a wrestler in college, and I think he ate all of his opponents — that she couldn't zip it up or let the sleeves out full length without making herself look like the daughter of the abominable snowman, so she just bunched the sleeves up above her elbows and pulled the two sides of it across each other, holding them in place. She was walking away from me, slowly, and from behind still didn't look quite like herself. More like a little bear, searching for some place to hibernate.

I wouldn't mind going to sleep for a few months, I think. At least until school is out. But by the time the comedians have gotten their last bruises, I'm still out in the hallway, wide awake and not feeling very good. I take a deep breath and go into the room.

"Robert?"

He looks up. Smiles. Changes his mind. His mouth instead goes straight across his face, underlining his eyes, which look sort of wary. "Hello."

"Can I talk to Robert for a while?" I ask.

He shrugs.

"I want to talk to you about Mrs. Cronski's class."

The smile comes back. "You were terrific. Better than anything I've ever done." He's impressed. Just what I was afraid of.

"But I got in trouble."

"No you didn't, Eleanor Roosevelt got in trouble."

"Well, then how come it's going on *my* school record and not *hers?*"

He shakes his head. "All that doesn't mean anything. What's important is that you did it."

"Well," I say and take another breath, "I'm not going to do it anymore. Not in a class, not in the cafeteria, not anywhere."

"Tut, tut, my good woman. Parents, eh? Don't worry. They'll get over it. Then things will be back to normal," he says, puffing out his stomach and sounding like one of his professor characters.

"Robert, please? My parents don't have anything to do with it. I decided on my own."

He frowns, then takes one of his mallets and lets it bounce off a bar. The note floats around the room, then comes back to the bar of wood and slowly fades back inside it. "And they didn't say anything about . . . me?"

"Nothing."

That surprises him a little. "So what's the problem? Why won't you do it anymore?"

"I told you. I got in trouble. I had to phone Mrs. Cronski last night and apologize."

"Yeeewwww," he goes, like I just told him he stepped in something awful. Then he scrapes the bottom of his shoe against a desk leg.

I have to laugh. "Cut it out."

"Listen, I have the perfect solution." A professor again. "You just won't do it in class again. That doesn't mean you have to quit."

"No. Robert? You just don't get it. We've been doing it too much. We get carried away. Robert, it's not good to get carried away all the time. What happened in Mrs. Cronski's class wasn't my idea. It's like I stopped thinking, just like with Van and Jimmy. Eleanor Roosevelt just appeared and said, 'Okay, Lisa's not doing so well here, so I'm going to sit in for a while.' "

But Robert's not listening. He's too busy getting excited. "But that's the best part, when you don't plan on it. The fun part."

I shake my head. "I don't want to be somebody without thinking about it first anymore. What happened in Mrs. Cronski's class might happen again."

"So? You didn't want to look stupid, did you?"

"I would have lived," I say. "I think." I shrug. "Anyway, it wouldn't have been the first time."

"But why look stupid if you don't have to?" He's getting upset with me now.

"I'm still not going to do it anymore," I say. "I don't want to hurt my grades."

"A chicken. A big chicken."

The word I've been waiting for. And now that he's said it, and even though it's true, I don't want to let him get away with it. "How would you know? You haven't done it. You didn't get sent down to the principal's office."

"I could handle it."

"Oh yeah? What about that first time I saw you in the social studies hallway with Jimmy? When Mr. Hummel threatened to send you down, you backed off."

His face turns red.

I've been seeing that color a lot lately.

Robert looks at me for a bit, then he packs up his music and mallets. "A traitor," he says.

I wince. That's worse than "chicken." "Robert . . ."

"Clint Eastwood," he says, heading out of the room.

"Clint . . ."

"Humphrey Bogart," he says, disappearing around the door.

I run after him. "Bogie . . ."

"Errol Flynn."

I give up. I lean against a locker and watch him go. Well, he didn't laugh at me. But that's not much consolation. He's angry and disappointed with me and I'm afraid he'll never say so much as hi to me again, even if he becomes my chivalrous Sir Walter Raleigh.

Morning classes are a blur. And lunchtime is lousy. I don't feel I'm anybody. I don't even feel I'm me. For a while there I lose it, put ketchup on my knife and walk around as Jack the Ripper, looking for a victim. I decide the ladies who prepare the food have been asking for it for a long time. I go up to one, holding the handle against my stomach with the blade pointing out. She sees me and says, "Don't fall like that or the handle will poke right into your intestines."

After that I'm okay, but I still could be better. The day just drags on. The special electricians the school hires to slow down the clocks in the classrooms are on overtime today. Every time I look at one I'd swear the minute hand moves backwards. On top of that, the first good weather in a long time puts in an appearance outside. I haven't heard birds singing all winter and all of a sudden fifty million of them open up at once, gathered under the window next to my desk. I can hardly hear my English teacher.

I manage to escape the general cheeriness of the day when I get to gym class. If you're ever depressed and you're not in the mood to be around happy people or a flock of birds, go to a locker room. I don't know how the gym teachers can stand to have their offices in there. If the smell isn't bad enough, you've got about forty girls telling what happened in all their classes up to that point all at the same time. Sometimes the lockers vibrate with the noise. And at the end of class, you have to stare at forty sweaty butts trying to pack into the showers at once so everybody can be sure to have enough time left to dry their hair. The way I'm feeling, it all suits me fine.

But good things always have to end. I'm the last one to straggle out of the locker room, and waiting just for me at a hallway window is the sun. It jumps straight into my eyes as soon as I appear, saying, "Ha ha, Lisa! It's still nice and wonderful out! I may even call in a few butterflies!" Who needs it?

I don't hear about Robert until my last class of the day, biology.

The class is a killer today. Why? I'll tell you. Despite the fact that I dissect eighteen hundred frogs, read seven thousand pages in my textbook, and write up a lab report that would win the Nobel Prize for length, if there ever were such a thing, when I get done and look at the clock I discover that only five minutes have gone by. Aargh!

That's when a girl who's seen me with Robert comes over and asks if I've heard what happened. She's in his math class, and right in the middle Robert got sent out of the room.

He was Pythagoras.

After that it only gets worse. As the week goes by, I keep hearing about Robert being sent to the office for disrupting just about all of his classes. The only one he doesn't do anything in is Mrs. Cronski's. I'm sure if he did Mrs. Cronski would figure we were in on it together and send us both to Mr. Ott.

Even the lunchrooms and hallways aren't safe from him, he gets yanked out of them all. The only time I actually see him do something he gets in trouble for is during assembly in the auditorium. When Mr. Mann stands to speak, Robert stands. Robert is, of course, also Mr. Mann. When Mr. Mann tells him to be quiet and sit down, Robert tells Mr. Mann to be quiet himself, that he's using up a lot of oxygen by talking and that the school can't afford any more until next term. The kids go berserk, laughing and throwing things around the auditorium. When Robert sits, Mr. Hummel lifts him right out of his chair and marches him out.

Robert, after a while, not only gets the World Series talk and the Super Bowl talk, he gets the Professional Wrestler's talk, which Mrs. Cronski has never even heard of before. I know because I ask her. Finally, the Monday after Easter, he gets the paddle.

By the middle of April, he gets suspended.

I start a brand-new habit, nail biting. The closest I ever came to developing a bad habit before this was when I got into brushing my hair at the dinner table. That started after I read a magazine article debating the usefulness of lots of brushing in order to gain a healthy scalp. I decided to brush a lot for a while, then do no brushing at all and see if I noticed a difference. I did it at the dinner table because that seemed to be the only time when I wasn't doing anything else. Except for eating. My parents put up with it for a while. Then one night my dad said, "Ah! Spaghetti for dinner. Now all I need is the meatballs and sauce." And when I looked over at him he had a glob of my hair on his fork. That was the end of the experiment.

"Honey, you're *ruining* your lovely hands," Mom says, irritated. Ever since I got in trouble she's kept me, every *part* of me, under a microscope.

I don't answer. Instead my right hand flies to my mouth and I start munching down heavily, like a rabbit in a carrot patch. Pretty soon I'll be down to my knuckles. I realize having no fingers might hurt my chances of getting into the space program, but maybe by then they'll have invented replacement hands made out of rubber. I wonder what rubber fingernails taste like.

Cody, the few times he ever loses interest in his school stuff and comes to me, I shove away. I just don't care, even when he starts whining. One night he sticks the cucumber in my face one too many times. I snatch it away from him and won't give it back. When he sees I'm going to keep it from him he does something I've never seen him do before. He rolls back his head and opens his mouth wide, the way he does when he's crying at full tilt. Only nothing comes out. It's as though I'm looking at a poster of Cody instead of the real thing. I could tack him right up next to my picture of Cape Canaveral. He keeps standing there without moving, I can't even see him breathe. Then something horrible happens.

One little tear leaks out of the corner of his eye and rolls down the side of his face. It does a detour at his collarbone and heads for the center of his chest, where it disappears inside his shirt. I look at him for a long time, but that's it, no more tears. I look at his bare feet, expecting at any moment for that one tear to come rolling out his pants leg. It's as though the last bit of life has popped out of Cody's eye to wander around his body, lost and lonely. And once it goes into his shirt I get the weird feeling I'll never see him again. I panic.

"Cody! Cody! Stop it this minute! Don't *do* that." I shake him to make him stop, and just like that he turns and walks out of the room.

After a while I remember the cucumber is still in my

hand. It looks like a giant green finger. I've been nibbling on the end.

Shortly after Robert gets suspended we have a visitor after dinner. I open the door, with my third finger for dessert in my mouth, to find Mrs. Wormer standing there.

"Hello, Lisa."

"Mrs. Wormer." I don't know whether to let her in or not. I'm not in the mood to have her finger in my face as well as my own. Then I think maybe she's joined a charity.

"Are you collecting for something?" I ask. If she is I can tell her we don't have any money and close the door on her.

"Your mother is expecting me," she says.

My mother. I don't have any choice. "Come on in." She steps up off the stoop and comes in, looking a lot larger than I remember her.

Mom hears our voices and comes down the hall as I'm shutting the door. "Betty, how nice to see you."

Betty?

"Hello, Lisa."

My mom's name is Lisa, too. It gets confusing. When they're just home together my parents call each other by their normal names, Mom and Dad. But if company shows up I practically twist my head off trying to keep track of who's trying to talk to me and who to my mom. On the phone it's worse: "Lisa?"

"Yes," I'll say.

"Have you heard that Ethel Duff is going to have surgery to have her breasts enlarged?"

"Who?"

Then it hits them. "Oh . . . oh, *Lisa*. I'm so sorry. Could you put your mother on? Oh, I'm sorry, Lisa. Just forget what I said."

I don't know what they think information like that will do to me, or even why they think it's important enough to get embarrassed about. I did look down at my chest on that one occasion, wondering why Mrs. Duff needed anything extra. She was already *way* ahead of me.

Mom and Mrs. Wormer go into the living room. I hang out by the doorway, waiting. Mom turns to me. "I'll see you later."

My mouth falls open. Here I am thinking this whole meeting is going to involve me and Mom sends me away. And as soon as I know I'm not wanted there I start wanting to be wanted. Up in my room I squirm around on my bed, trying to do homework. Every time a laugh leaps up the stairway I lift my head and strain to hear. But their voices always drop back below teenager range and leave me there wondering.

After an hour Mom unexpectedly calls, "Lisa? Would you like some dessert with us?"

I look at my third finger. I've pretty much finished it off, and I don't think there are many calories in a fingernail anyway. I go downstairs.

I look in the den on my way to the kitchen. Dad and Cody have been playing horsy. Dad has his face buried in the deep pile carpeting. He's either being a very convincing horse and is grazing on the floor or he's asleep, with his rear end up in the air. Cody is asleep on top.

In the kitchen Mom has a pan of her brownies in the middle of the table and is passing around plates. Mrs. Wormer looks red around the eyes.

"How are you, Lisa?" she asks.

As soon as she opens her mouth I forget the brownies and a new finger dives for cover between my front teeth.

Mrs. Wormer says, "I know you must be almost as upset about Robert as I am, being his friend. I thought you might know . . . why he's doing this?"

I just sit there.

"Don't you have *any* idea?" asks Mom.

I look at her and shake my head. Her lips roll up into each other and she looks helplessly at Mrs. Wormer.

"Lisa, your mother tells me you had a little trouble in your history class." Now I know what they were talking about in the living room. It *did* have to do with me, only they just wanted to get their facts straight before they gave me the third degree. Mom must be reading my mind. She gets up to turn off the overhead light in the kitchen and turns on the little one hanging right over the table. It shines right into my eyes. I start to fidget.

It slips out. "You can't make me talk, coppers." James Cagney. I learned that one from Robert.

"What? *What did you say?*" says Mom, getting steamed. "You said you weren't . . ."

Mrs. Wormer puts a hand on her arm. "Maybe I should talk to her a few minutes alone."

Uh-oh.

After a second or two, Mom stands and walks out without looking at me. I'm all alone.

"Lisa, you like to make believe, don't you?"

I don't say anything.

"I think that's fine . . . for children. But you're grown up. Don't you think it's time to leave make-believe behind?"

I don't say anything.

"You're at an age when young adults start trying on different roles, but not in a make-believe sense. You shouldn't be trying to be *other* people, just yourself. You should be reflecting on what your beliefs and values might be and interacting with other kids doing the same thing. It may be that your beliefs will turn out to be different from your parents'," she says, smiling a little bit. "Your mom probably wouldn't want me saying that. But it's true. That's part of becoming an individual. You might not understand all that I'm saying, I'm afraid."

I don't, but I'm not going to admit it.

"My point is, Robert is not doing what he should be doing." She looks down at the uneaten brownie in front of her. "I guess we haven't been the best of parents to him."

She can say *that* again.

"His father is very much devoted to the military. Robert is not. Has Robert ever told you his father has always planned for him to go to school at a military academy?"

I shake my head no.

"I guess that's what got Robert started in all this. He's had several friends over the years who've wanted to make believe with him. Fewer recently. I thought he would finally stop it at this age after he ran out of people to do it with. Then, he met you. Now he won't even quit when he's around me." She looks at me and reaches for her purse.

This is it!

But instead of a gun she pulls out a Kleenex, dabs at her nose.

I sigh and sink back in my chair.

"What happened?" she asks. "Did somebody, a teacher, make Robert really mad?"

I keep thinking about how I accused him of backing down in front of Mr. Hummel, suggesting that he was just as big a chicken as me, and the more I do, the more I'm convinced it sounded like I was challenging him to prove me wrong. I hold my breath, waiting for her to somehow guess this.

"It's gotten to the point where we really have to do something, or he'll be thrown out of school for good. He's going to have to learn to give up his make-believe. Or else he's just going to hurt himself."

She gets up and I brace myself to scream at the first move she makes to rush around and reach for my throat, shouting, "It was you! You did this to him!"

But she just stares at me. "Don't you have anything to say to me about him? At all?"

Not a thing.

But the longer she stares the more uncomfortable I get. Is she just going to stay here until I answer? Where's Mom? Isn't it about my bedtime? Where's Dad? Oh, yeah, out to pasture with Cody.

My bottom is going numb on the chair. I want to change my position, but Mrs. Wormer has got me nailed in place with her eyes. Maybe she's trying to put me in a trance and get me to talk that way. Then after she's heard everything she'll be too mad to kill me. She'll just make me a zombie slave for the rest of my life, make me walk around blindly with my arms stretched out in front of me, saying, "Yes, master, yes, master."

"Lisa? Are you all right?"

"Hunh?" I look up at her.

"Your eyes glazed over."

"Oh. No, I'm fine."

She stares a while longer, not looking too convinced. Suddenly, quietly, she says, "Well, I have to go," and carries her plate to the sink. "Good night, Lisa. I do hope you'll continue to be his friend. I think you're probably the best he's had." She pauses by the kitchen door, then she goes down the hall and has a few more words with my mom.

I can't believe she let me off so easily. She didn't yell once. In fact, she didn't act at all the way she did over at Robert's that first day. She seemed more like . . . *my* mom. Did she really mean that I'm the best friend he's ever had?

Mom steps back into the kitchen. She looks like she's going to explode. Now I see — Mrs. Wormer and Mom have changed places. "Please don't turn into the old Mrs. Wormer," I mutter.

"What?" she snaps. When I don't answer, she says, "Lisa, I'm disappointed in you. She was more understanding than any normal person in her predicament has a right to be, and here you were unable to tell her anything at all. I find that hard to believe, considering how close you and Robert have been. What's gotten into you? For a while now you've just been moody and cranky and — *stop* biting your fingernails! I swear I don't know what to do with you anymore."

The feeling is mutual.

✦11✦

I'm tired of Mom. I'm tired of Dad. I'm tired of Cody. I'm tired of Van and even of me. And before Mother's Day rolls around, Robert gets suspended another time.

Once more and he gets expelled.

He won't let me talk to him. I haven't been able to since we were in the music room. I'm not even another person to him anymore. I'm not even another *animal*. I'm like a garden wall, or a ship deck, or a rock beside a pond, just a thing that's in the background for whoever he decides to be at the time.

After his third suspension, I finally break down and go up to Van at her locker one day. "I need you to do me a favor."

She turns and I follow her into the girls' bathroom. She waits until there's nobody else in there. "What?" she says. She's still wearing her dad's sweaters.

"I want you to pass Robert a note in Mrs. Cronski's class telling him to meet you during lunch in the alley behind the school that leads to the cafeteria kitchen. Only instead of you, it'll be me that meets him.''

"Anything else?"

I look at her. "You're not going to do it, are you?"

"Why should I?"

"Because I'm trying to keep Robert from getting himself expelled."

Van sniffs. "Doesn't matter to me. Just one less of the ENEMY to deal with."

"Knock it off!" I yell.

"Knock what off?" she yells back.

We don't say anything else for a bit, calming down. I ask, "Why is Robert so particularly bad?"

She rolls her eyes. "Come on. Just look at all the trouble he's gotten into."

"That doesn't answer my question," I say. "What do *you* find so wrong with him?"

"I *did* answer your question. I find wrong with him what everybody else finds wrong with him. He always pretends to be somebody else, usually somebody who was great. Well, he's *not* those other people, and he's *not* great. He's just Robert Wormer. So why doesn't he just *be* Robert Wormer?"

"Why don't you just *be* Vandelle Barnsdorf, then?" I ask.

"Hunh?"

"Why do you dye your hair green? And wear all those safety pins and torn clothes?"

"Because I'm an individual. *That* ought to be clear even to you. I'm making a statement about women in general and me specifically. That we can dress how we want, when we want, and should not be discriminated against for it.''

"Then why are you wearing that sweater?" I ask softly.

She takes the two sides and wraps them tighter around her. "I'm cold. It's cold out these days. Usually happens in the wintertime.''

"It's spring, Van. The days are getting warmer, not colder.''

"Well, maybe I'm having trouble with my body's internal thermostat. How should I know? I'm just cold, that's all.''

"Van, it's okay if you're worried about . . . how heavy you are . . .''

"I'm not worried.''

"Then what about what you said in the hall the other day?"

"I don't remember what I said.''

"*Van*. You pretend just as much as Robert does.''

"What!" She's shouting again.

"You do. It's like my mother said . . .''

"*Oh*, your *mother*. She doing your thinking for you now?"

"*No*," I say, starting to get angry. "Why don't you admit that you wear those clothes to cover up your weight.''

"I do not!''

"You pretend you can be this great feminist when you really wish you were slim and could date boys like anybody else!''

"You're crazy!''

"But that's not the worst part. The worst part isn't pretending that. The worst part is pretending . . . Van . . . is pretending not to like me.'' I start to cry.

"I *don't* like you," she says, squeezing out a few tears herself.

"You do too."

"I don't!"

"You do. And I think that's the worst thing you could ever do to somebody who considered you a friend. A best friend."

She doesn't say anything to that. The tears sort of dry up on both of us and we just stand there breathing hard with our faces flushed.

A girl comes in after it's been quiet a while. "Can I use a toilet now?"

"Get out!" bellows Van.

"But it's my period," the girl whines, crossing her legs. She has on some new white pants. Even Van knows what it means to have a combination of white pants and your period. Van nods and the girl goes scurrying into a stall.

Van glances at me and tugs at her sweater. "I'll give him the note," she says, and starts to walk away.

"It hurt, Van," I say, still a little choked up.

"I'll give him the note," she repeats without turning around.

"It hurt," I say, but she's gone.

She passes the note to him in history. But I don't find out if he's agreed to do it or not until I see Van later in the hallway. All she does is nod and walk on.

I leave the building late, wanting Robert to be there before me. When I turn the corner I'm surprised to see that Van has shown up, too, though I didn't ask her to. She's standing with Robert, and both stop talking when they see me.

"Come on," Robert says to Van, and starts to go around me.

I step in his way so he has no choice but to stop. That's why I chose the alley. He can't get by me, so he'll have to stop and listen. The inside door to the cafeteria kitchen is open, but the screen door is shut and locked to keep kids who've been cutting class from sneaking back into school.

"This is a private conversation," says Robert when he can't get by me.

"I told Van to give you the note," I say.

He doesn't believe me. He looks at Van, who just stares back at him without speaking. When he sees it's true he sneers. "So now what?"

"I just want to talk to you about . . . maybe getting expelled."

"What's to say? I'm going to get expelled, big deal."

"Don't you understand? You'll get thrown out of school. They won't let you back in."

"I'll just be put in another school. One is the same as the next."

"And once you're in another school you'd just do this all over again? Suspension and all?"

He shrugs.

"Robert, how can you not care?"

He surprises me by putting a finger in my face, looking an awful lot like his mom. "I told you I could handle it. The school, classes, kids . . . they're there for me and my friends." I wonder what friends he's talking about, and then I figure out "friends" means all the people he pretends to be. "Teachers and administrators, they can't talk to Robert Wormer because I won't let them. All they can do is argue

144

with whoever I choose to be at the time. It's fantastic! You should see the looks on their faces. They don't know what to do. They can't *make* me be Robert Wormer. It drives them nuts.''

"But you didn't get in trouble like this before," I say. "Why are you doing this all of a sudden? Is . . . is it because of me?''

"Ha!" he laughs, but it doesn't sound real. "Is that why you're here? To say you're sorry and make me feel better? Well, just go away, take off. I do what I do because I want to.''

I don't believe him. He never before went out of his way to get himself in trouble, and the whole time we were . . . partners in pretending . . . he didn't even insist a teacher call him Charles, the way he did his first day in history class.

I feel I've deserted him, left him alone again with Abraham Lincoln, George Custer, and others who are exciting to bring alive but who *aren't* alive and can never listen to Robert and joke with him the way I can. Or could. Left him to prove to me that he's fearless, a quality I've never doubted in him, never needed proof of.

"But you're just hurting yourself," I say, hearing myself plead with him. And thinking, "You're hurting me, too."

"That's what you don't get," he says, reasoning with me. "That's what Robert's tried to show you all along. He never gets upset, he never has to worry. He can always escape when trouble comes along. They can't touch him. *They can't touch him.*''

I look helplessly at Van. But she just stands there, watching and listening. I look back at Robert. Getting expelled.

That has to be bad even for him. Doesn't it? What would his parents do with him? Put him in another school? And then another? And another? Would his father finally force him to go into a military academy?

I can't help myself. It's crazy, but in the midst of developing new worry wrinkles across my forehead, I have to fight back a smile. Suddenly I'm picturing Robert as John Wayne telling some military instructor to form the class into a circle to hold off the Indians.

"What's so funny?" asks Robert.

I shake my head. "You are," I have to say, giggling, or else I'll bust a gut.

He smiles a little, hopeful. "That's me! Better than Ringling Brothers!"

"I almost wish I could . . ." I start to say.

"Could what?" he asks.

"I almost wish I could be Eleanor Roosevelt all over again," I say. I glance at Van, but she still doesn't say anything.

"My deah," he says with his British accent, "anything is pos-sible. Hmmm?"

I shake my head, hopelessly. "I can't, Robert. I just can't. Lisa Archer won't let me." I don't know what else to say. I need the cavalry to come riding up armed with some useful advice.

Instead, I get Jimmy Pinto and his gang, on foot and without white hats. "All my favorite friends," he says, sauntering up to us. The three guys behind him smile dangerously.

Robert looks at me, sighs, and steps forward to get this over with. A big smile comes over his face. "Back for another try, eh, Jim? I'll tell you what, if you've got an electric watch . . .''

Monty Hall again.

But Jimmy cuts him off. "My buddies say you're just putting me on all the time."

Robert takes out his wallet, bored. "Here's the five-dollar bill, Mr. Pinto. Just waiting to leap into your pocket."

Jimmy snatches the money from his hand.

Robert is startled for a moment, but he recovers.

"Ah-ah-ah. Mustn't be greedy. All contestants must play by the rules." He reaches for the bill, but Jimmy knocks his hand away.

I feel myself getting scared. Typical. I tell myself to calm down, to just wait. In a minute Robert will take control.

"Putting me on? Putting me on? You think that's a fun thing to do around me? Hunh?" says Jimmy.

Robert puts his hands on his hips, impatient. "I'm actually bending the rules a little here, Jim. Most of our audience members come dressed in costume. What you're wearing doesn't have much imagination in it at all."

One of the guys grabs my arms from behind, the other two restrain Van. Just as I start to figure out why, Jimmy punches Robert in the stomach.

And I scream.

Jimmy steps back, waiting for Robert to retaliate. That's what he's used to and his hands are up defensively. But Robert stays crumpled over, leaning against the wall and breathing hard. After a few seconds Jimmy drops his hands.

"That was easy," he says, satisfied. "Guess you know now you can play class clown for anybody else but me.

147

Right, Worm Hole?'' Jimmy backs away, still wary but starting to relax. All of a sudden he stops and cranes his head. Taking a step forward, he asks, ''What? What did you say?''

Though I can't hear anything, Robert seems to be speaking. I struggle to get closer, but the kid holding me tightens his grip.

''What?'' Jimmy repeats, maybe thinking that Robert is just gasping for air.

''I'm . . .'' replies Robert, louder now. ''I'm . . . Leonardo da Vinci.''

Jimmy's head snaps back, as though Robert has come up and clipped him on the chin. He turns, puzzled, to his friends. I see one guy holding Van shrug.

''What?'' demands Jimmy, more alarmed than anything else.

Robert stands a little straighter. ''Leonardo da Vinci. I paint. Sometimes do a little wallpapering.''

Jimmy squints at Robert. Again he looks to his buddies for support.

''He's doing it to you again, Jim,'' the one behind me says. ''He's mouthing off.''

Jimmy immediately holds a fist in front of Robert's face. ''Knock it off, Worm Hole. Understand me?''

''Da Vinci's the name. You've heard of my girlfriend, Mona?''

Jimmy licks his lips. After a final glance at the rest of us, he halfheartedly socks Robert again in the same place. The air goes out of Robert and he doubles over even farther than before.

''Stop all your yapping. You just sound stupid. If you

want to be a big man in front of your girlfriends, shut up and come at me.'' Jimmy beckons to Robert, looking hopeful.

But as soon as Robert recovers, he says, "I'm Albert Einstein.''

Jimmy looks as though he feels trapped. Robert's not giving in, but he's also not trying to punch it out with him. Jimmy's friends shift uncomfortably. One of them coughs.

"You are a worm hole!" Jimmy's voice cracks. "Say it. You're a worm *hole*.''

"I'm Albert Einstein.''

This time Jimmy hits him in the face.

"Don't!" I shout. I still can't shake free.

"I'm Winston . . .''

Jimmy doesn't let him finish, but Robert won't stop.

"Winston Church —''

Jimmy hits him again. And again and again. One punch for each wrong name Robert gives him.

"I'm not going to let up until you say it, so say it!" Jimmy chokes on his words and his face reddens. His hands are shaking. "Well?''

"I'm Benjamin Franklin.''

Jimmy lets out a frustrated cry and at the same time lights into Robert with both hands.

"Say! What's going on out there?" A bright white apron with the outline of a woman's head on top appears behind the dark screen of the cafeteria kitchen door. Then it disappears.

"Come on, Jimmy, she's going for help.''

"Say it!" Now Jimmy is almost sobbing. Robert gets too heavy for the wall to hold up, and he finally slides down into a sitting position. Jimmy reaches down and grabs him

149

by the collar. In a hoarse whisper comes a final "Say it."

There's a lot of commotion going on in the kitchen now and Jimmy's three friends rush past me and Van and haul him away from Robert. As we pass each other going in opposite directions, I notice tears on Jimmy's cheeks.

Mr. Hummel, on lunch patrol duty, bursts through the kitchen door first, just as Jimmy goes around the corner out of sight. He finds Van kneeling beside Robert, with me standing right behind.

"You again," says Mr. Hummel, squatting beside Robert. He says to Van, "Go to the nurse's station. Bring her here. I don't want to move him till she has a look." Van leaves. "You," he says to me, "can go down to the front office and bring back Mr. Ott, or whoever's available." He looks back at Robert. "What a mess."

I can't move. There's this voice going on inside my head. It's been there for a while, and now that everyone has stopped moving around in front of my eyes, I can hear it. It's saying, "Be somebody! Be somebody!" Only it's not talking to me, it's talking to Robert. I keep expecting him to jump up, wipe the bruises from his face, and smile. But he doesn't do it. "Be somebody!" it says. But he just keeps lying there with his eyes closed.

"Come on, girl, what are you waiting for?" asks Mr. Hummel, looking up at me. *"Go."*

That sinks in. I take a couple of wobbly steps. A couple more. The door to the kitchen seems so far away.

"What? What's that?"

I think Mr. Hummel is talking to me and I go back. Looking over his shoulder I see it's Robert he's listening to, Robert who is trying to talk.

"What's that?" asks Mr. Hummel.

"Worm Hole," says Robert. "Worm. Hole."

I go through the kitchen and up the main hallway. I go past the offices and straight out the front door. When I get to Farm Road, which runs out in front of the school, I walk down it until I get to a public bus stop. I get on the first bus that comes by.

I don't know how long I ride around. I stay in the rear of the bus where the driver won't notice me and ask why I'm not getting off anywhere. I close my eyes. "Be somebody," the voice keeps saying. I open my eyes again.

There's a bag lady sitting across the aisle from me with all her shopping bags arranged around her like little children. She even goes around to them all, patting whatever's on top like she would pat a kid's head, and talks to them. She takes out a bureau mirror, a plastic one like the kind I had when I was about five, that's all blue and yellow and comes to a swirl on top that finishes in a rose blossom. She looks into it and pats the gray curls at the side of her head and adjusts her stocking cap.

"Be somebody," the voice says in my head. "Go away," I tell it.

I just want to be quiet and still, watch how she touches every inch of her face with her fingers, seeing if anything's different from this morning when she last looked into it. They're such gentle touches, now down around her chin and along the side of her jaw. I think it would be nice to have those hands tuck me in at night or hold a damp washcloth to my head when I have a fever.

"Hey, kid," says this sarcastic voice. "You and your mom getting off any time today?"

I turn and see the bus is empty except for the lady and me. The bus driver is looking in his big mirror back at us. I stand to go out the rear exit. I happen to look down as I leave. The lady hasn't heard him. She's still looking in the mirror. And for the first time I see the mirror doesn't have any glass.

I catch another bus that goes across town. This time I keep an eye on how many people are on there with me. It stays pretty full, so after a while I just lay my head against the window and watch all the buildings slide by. When the bus comes to a stop in front of the hospital, I realize this is where I have meant to come all along.

I'm practically inside Cody's classroom and making a beeline across the floor to him before I think to make up a story for why I'm here. I only get to rehearse it once before I'm up next to Mrs. Jenkins.

"Why, Lisa! What are you doing here?" Mrs. Jenkins stands.

"Mrs. Jenkins, my mom's waiting in the car. We have to take Cody out early today."

"Why? What's wrong?"

"Well, we forgot, but he has to take some tests today."

"Tests? What kind of tests?"

"Well, we're kind of late for them now and I really don't have time to explain, but we have to get him to the hospital."

That's when I realize that I've made one slight mistake.

Mrs. Jenkins cocks her head a little to the side. "What hospital?"

"Not this one," I say, trying to fix things. "The other one. Across town."

"Why does he have to go there?"

"A specialist," I say. I try to remember some of the types of doctors Cody's been to over the years. My mind goes blank. "A numismatist," I say.

"A what?" She cocks her head a little more.

"Well, I don't remember what he does, but my mom *is* waiting."

"Maybe I should go talk to your mother . . ."

"But she's not around."

"You said she was waiting in the car."

"She's waiting in the car in the parking garage across the street. Way up top. It'll take a long time to walk up there."

Mrs. Jenkins's head lowers sideways another inch. It's like a hot air balloon losing its air and slowly sagging over to the ground. "Well, if she's parked, why didn't she come in here herself?"

"She knew that I could get here faster. I ran over, see? We're awfully late, Mrs. Jenkins."

"Then why did she bother parking in the garage? If she's in a hurry she should have waited on the street."

Somehow my story has gotten totally away from me, and Mrs. Jenkins's head looks as though it's going to fall off her neck any second the way she's looking at me. I'm desperate to get it going back up again. "She was robbed once, when she was waiting on the street. A guy came by on the sidewalk, reached in, grabbed her purse, and ran away."

Mrs. Jenkins's head wavers a bit, goes up a half inch. "That's terrible."

"Yes," I say. Trying to add to the tragedy, and remembering the night Mrs. Wormer came over to visit with her trancelike eyes, I say, "He was a zombie."

That does it. Mrs. Jenkins's head loses the half-inch gain and will probably never rise again on its own. They'll have to get a tow truck in here to lift it back.

"He was *dressed* like a zombie," I say, panicky. "He was on his way to a party."

A miracle. Mrs. Jenkins straightens her head without any help. Maybe she was robbed by a guy dressed like a zombie once herself.

"Lisa. I think I'd better phone your mother."

"But . . . but she's . . ."

"You wait right here. And we'll find out why you aren't in school."

I stand there, speechless, as Mrs. Jenkins walks over to a wall phone.

·12·

Mrs. Jenkins turns her back for just a second.

I reach down and grab Cody, getting him halfway to the door before I see that he's still attached to Mad Martin. The motorcycle is lying in a variety of pieces, like a trail of bread crumbs, stretching from us back to the corner of the room where they were playing.

"Let go of him, Cody!" I say, trying to pry his fingers loose from Martin's shirt. Up to this point nobody's noticed us because Cody figured what I was doing was somehow part of today's lesson, but as soon as I start working on his grip he lets out a howl. All eyes turn to us.

"Lisa!" Mrs. Jenkins drops the phone and rushes over.

At the same time, I get Cody to turn Martin loose. I lift him up and head for the door at full speed. Behind me, Martin starts to cry. In sympathy all the other kids start crying, too, and as I sprint into the hallway their sad voices follow me, echoing down the long hall.

My luck improves after that. I get to a bus just as it's ready to pull away. I sit down and look out in time to see

155

Mrs. Jenkins waving at me frantically and shouting. Fortunately, to the bus driver she just looks like another pedestrian who got to the stop a little too late. We pull away and leave her in an exhale of bus smoke.

Cody settles down once we're on the bus. He likes buses and he starts checking everything out, the passing scenery, the passengers, the interesting colors of gum stuck to the seat back in front of us. I notice a few stares, so I pull up the hood on Cody's sweat shirt and tie it in place so his face is obscured. After that he looks like a periscope, swiveling for a look here and there, finally isolating a Zondarian who's already paid a trip to the Mighty Mart and is now on a little sea voyage before she returns to her home asteroid.

"Pazzuh! Pazzuh!"

Torpedoes one and two are away.

The bus comes to a jarring stop to let an ambulance whiz by. The woman clutching the grocery bags sways and grabs her bags tighter. Like magic, a seam opens up on one of them.

"A direct hit!" I whisper to Cody. He comes up to periscope depth for a better look.

A bag of white rice slowly squeezes halfway out the opening, looking like some animal's guts.

"Aw-w-w-w," says Cody.

"I agree. Pretty disgusting. That Zondarian must have her pet Gronk in there."

The bag of rice drops free. Next comes an apple.

"The heart," I say.

And another apple.

"I didn't know Gronks had two," I say with a little surprise.

And a head of lettuce, which makes the hole even bigger.

"Green brains. That figures. Only a Zondarian would have a pet with green brains."

By that time the lady catches on, but she only becomes flustered and grabs the bag in the worst kind of way, spilling everything else out onto the floor.

"Sighted sack, sank same." I congratulate Cody, shaking his hand.

Since the bus we're on is heading in the wrong direction, we have to make a couple of transfers. Cody tries a few more naval maneuvers, including cruising up and down the aisle for a likely target, but nothing matches his initial success.

Ever since the ambulance went by I've been aware of sirens. Any second I expect a police cruiser to pull the bus over and to see Mrs. Jenkins come leaping out. "That's her, officer! She stole her brother right out of my class." The officer will shake his head sadly. "Brother-napping, hunh? Don't you know you get the death penalty for that?" Mom and Dad will plead with the judge for mercy, but he won't listen. They'll haul me off, tie my wrists together, and slowly lower me into a brown, boiling vat of peanut butter.

Peanut butter?

I start to feel a little shaky, and it's a relief when we finally get home.

Cody totters up the walk to the front door, excited to be home at this strange hour. I open the door and let him in. Close it behind me. Now all the world is gone. There's just me and Cody. With my back leaning against the door I announce to the empty house, "Commander Coatrack returns!"

I start flinging coats and hats off the rack, working myself down to the bare bones. When I'm done I lift it up off the floor. "Okay, launch in five minutes."

No Cody.

I set the rack down and find him in the living room. With his school things! "Hey," I say, "what's the big idea? Let's go, you're going to miss your flight."

Cody runs his hands back and forth across some board with colors and shapes on it. He looks at me, smacking the board happily.

"No, no, no. You don't have to *do* that. Don't you get it? You're free! You can play with me now. Don't worry about that stuff. Come on. Come *on*." Getting him to let loose of the board is like trying to get him unattached from Martin. He starts to bawl.

"Okay," I say, "you can take it along with you. But remember, we can't have too many extra items or the spacecraft will be overloaded." I pick him up. Immediately one hand flies free of the board and lands on the arm of the sofa.

"Cody! What's the matter with you? Let go. Why do you want to stay here? There's nothing to do here! It's all out in the hallway. Don't you remember? You have to remember. Commander, you're the best! The universe depends on you." I pull on him and he pulls on the sofa. The sofa has nothing to pull on and starts to move away from the wall. I make little grunts. Cody makes little grunts. The sofa goes "Eee-ee-ee-orp," across the wooden floor.

I let go. Cody looks at me, his lower lip trembling. I will have to chop off the sofa arm before I can ever hope to bring him with me. Then I get an idea.

I run up to my room, scour my desk top, my book-shelves, dive into my closet to hunt among my boots and shoes. Under my bed I find it. It looks like a strangely shaped, green dust ball, but after I clean it off the cucumber looks pretty good.

Except for the hole I gnawed into one end.

Downstairs I hold it in front of Cody's face. ''Recognize this? Sure you do. It gives you the power to master all your enemies. Cody?'' His lower lip is still doing its job, twitch-ing as fast as a flickering light bulb just before it burns out.

''I don't understand.'' I lower the cucumber and hear a noise at my feet. I look down to see all the little dried cucumber seeds running out the end onto the floor. I used to tell him that the rattling noise they made was all the energy particles spinning around inside, waiting to be released whenever he wanted to blast something. Now they just make a little pile at my feet, just like the paper clips out of Van's ears.

The seeds are what finally get Cody's attention. He drops to the floor and starts picking them up. Seeing my chance, I drop the cucumber and pick him up, carrying him into the hallway. He starts this awful squalling right in my ear, getting me so upset I don't know what to do.

''I can't believe you're doing this to me. I've set you free! You can do whatever you want, not what that teacher wants you to do! Now, here's the ship. *Here.* Just sit there and I'll put it over you.'' I set him on the floor, but as soon as I let go of him he starts to crawl away. ''Cody!'' I grab the coatrack and lift it up, trying to capture him with it. ''Hold still! Hold still!''

I hit him in the head.

Everything is dead silent for a few seconds. Then, with the appearance of a little trickle of blood over his right eye, Cody starts screaming. I drop the coatrack and it crashes to the floor on its side.

"Oh, Cody, I'm sorry." I try to put my arms around him, but he fights me. "Cody, please, I'm sorry. Oh, Cody. Cody." The blood smears across his forehead, gets on my sleeves. When I get close enough he smacks me. In the face, in the neck. My tears start coming. "I just wanted you to be the Commander again. I wanted you to save the universe, Cody. I wanted you to save me. To save me."

This is when my mother comes home.

The front door flies open and she appears, her hair looking electrified from the wind and standing straight up, her spring coat unbuttoned. "Lisa! I couldn't believe it when Mrs. Jenkins called. Have you lost your mind?"

It must look that way. She faces coats on the floor, the coatrack on top of the coats, Cody sitting on the floor with his face covered with blood and making enough noise to wake the dead, and me crying, trying to reach him, trying to gather him up.

"Mom," is all I can say, crying, "Mom."

"What are you doing? Are you trying to kill him?" She rushes over to get to us, but the coatrack is in the way. She snatches it from the floor to set it upright. A top hook catches in her cuff while a middle hook snags the coat's belt loop. She can't get away from it.

First she tries to push it back into place against the wall. After that she just tries to back away from it, but it follows. Together they look like a couple dancing around and around in the hallway. Cody stops crying.

"I can't . . . it won't . . ."

The more Mom struggles the more the rack tries to lead the way. Cody starts to laugh. "Ahhhhhh."

The rack finally waltzes her against the wall and they come to a stop. The brass ball on top bends down and smacks her in the mouth, as though it's giving her a thank you kiss. Mom eyes us, sees Cody laughing, and figures then that he's not dying. She sags against the wall. "Help."

I get her free, mainly by having her slip out of her coat while it's still attached to the rack. When she steps back, the rack looks like a briar patch that managed to capture some hiker's clothes.

We take Cody upstairs. Mom closes the toilet and sits on the seat, making him stand in front of her. She doesn't talk to me except to ask for things. "Pass me his washcloth. Now some soap. Pass the Bactine. Band-Aids." With the blood gone he doesn't look so bad.

Afterward Cody is pretty agreeable to being put to bed for a nap.

Mom and I trudge downstairs to pick up. We leave her coat the way it is and bury it under all the other junk. At last we can push the coatrack back in place.

Mom slides down the wall to the floor and closes her eyes. I sit next to her. "I may not look or sound like it, but I'm still very upset."

I don't say anything.

"You want to tell me what's been going on?" She turns her head to me and opens her eyes.

I shrug.

"You don't know? You have no idea why you did what you did today?"

My next strategic move is to start biting my nails.

Mom sighs. "Okay. Listen. I'm sorry I burst in here like a wild woman."

"You asked if I'd lost my mind."

"Yes. Well, even if you have, I'm sure we can find it again."

"*Mother.*"

"All right. Jokes aside. I apologize for that, too."

"You asked if I was trying to kill Cody."

She doesn't say anything at first. "I know. I know. That was just plain stupid. I'm ashamed I said it. Forgive me?"

I grumble. "Yeah."

"Did I say anything else? I really don't remember." I shake my head. "Good. So, do you have something to say to me?"

I take a deep breath. And although I don't feel like this was all my fault I say, "I'm sorry I left school and everything. And made you worry about Cody."

She smiles a little. "Now. We're on equal footing, hmmm?"

I shrug.

"But you still can't explain what happened?"

I bite my nails.

Mom looks straight ahead. Glances at the coatrack. Looks back at me. "Let's start with the rack. What were you doing with it?"

"I was trying to get Cody underneath. I thought we could play."

"What happened?"

"He didn't want to. I tried to make him anyway . . . and I bumped him in the head."

"You couldn't get him to play with you?"

"No. He wanted to play with all his dumb school things. As usual."

"They're not dumb, Lisa. Cody likes school. I don't understand why you've been against him going."

"Because nobody asked me in the first place," I say. "You had him tested and everything without telling me. Then you sort of thought afterward, well, let's see what Lisa thinks. But you were all set to send him to school anyway, weren't you? Well, I think that stinks."

Mom nods her head, as though she should have known. "Dr. Barnes said we should involve you in the whole process . . ."

"Dr. *Barnes*. Dr. *Barnes*."

"You're not being fair to him, Lisa."

"Well, you're not being fair to me."

"You'd feel different if you met him. I guess that's my fault, too. Dad's wanted you to. But you've always been the one who never needed any help. It just seemed you'd be getting mixed up in a mess we made for ourselves. And as we've gotten out of that mess, and the plans came up for Cody . . . I don't know. It just seemed natural not to have to make you a part of that either."

"I don't want to be a part of it. Dr. Barnes has caused nothing but problems. I brought Cody home to play . . . but he *never* wants to play with me anymore. He spends all his time with you and his homework."

"Well, he finds that just as enjoyable. It satisfies him."

"Yeah, *him*. But what about me? I never have fun with him anymore."

"You sound like a little child, Lisa. Did you grab your

brother out of school just because you felt like playing with him?''

I slam myself back against the wall and don't say anything.

Mom sighs and puts her hand to her forehead. Her hair has de-electrified and collapsed in clumps all around her face. She tugs at her bangs. "I know there has to be more to it than that.''

"Why does there have to be? I wanted to be with Cody.''

"You couldn't wait until after school?''

"*You're* with him after school. That's the time when we'd usually be together.''

"Lisa, I can't believe you're serious. You're being unreasonable.''

"Mom, you didn't used to spend much time with him at all, so how do you know I'm being unreasonable?'' I'm so mad and hurt that it just slips out.

Mom stops playing with her bangs. Her face hardens. "Maybe I don't know. Does that mean you can't begrudge me a little while with him after school?''

"You have him more than a little while. Up until dinner. And then after dinner it's not surprising if he's back in the living room again.''

"I don't work with him after dinner. He just sometimes comes to sit in my lap and falls asleep while I read.''

"See? It doesn't matter. He's with you.''

"You're always welcome to come help with his schooling.''

"Mom, all I ever get to do is sit there and watch. Like a cheering section. Who wants to sit there listening to you

164

and Cody give milk together?'' She doesn't get my cow reference.

"Well, a lot of it *is* one-on-one type of work,'' she says. "To aid his concentration there should be just one person that he has to focus on.''

"You,'' I say.

"Mrs. Jenkins says it's best to be consistent in his instruction. A regular agenda is important.''

"So the answer is no. You won't let me.''

"It's not a question of not letting you.''

"Well, I don't see him really learning anything. His homework things look like toys to me. Those colored blocks and boards. You've substituted your games for mine and you're keeping him all to yourself. To punish me. To *punish* me. Well, what did I do?'' My voice cracks. "I took care of him. That's what I did. And now Dr. Barnes won't let me have him anymore.''

"No, Lisa, no.'' Mom looks as surprised as she did when she first came in the door. I almost expect her hair to stick back up again. She reaches out to take my shoulder, but her hand only gets halfway there. It freezes in the air, as though she's playing statues and that's how she stops.

A tear rolls down Mom's cheek, which surprises me. "You feel like I'm punishing you?'' She sniffs, and her hand retreats to wipe her own face. Then she folds her hands in her lap and looks down at them. She smiles a little. "I thought you were punishing me.''

I squint my eyes at her.

"What you said. About taking care of him. Just like a mother . . . just like I should have. Only I didn't. Then

165

when . . . we got on the right track, and I was ready to be his mother, I couldn't. You were already there. He didn't need me.''

I shake my head and my face burns. Why is she saying this? Why is she blaming me?

"I admitted something to myself once. Then I decided I was wrong, and I buried the thought, the way we buried my coat under all those other things on the rack. I . . . I've been jealous of you.''

My throat tightens. It tightens right up through my mouth and into my brain, strangling around my thoughts. I feel like Cody when the words come into his ears but they just don't make any sense.

"When Dr. Barnes suggested the testing, I didn't think too much about it. But when the results were so good, and we knew we could send Cody to school . . . it was all something new for Cody. He was beginning something. And I was so excited about beginning it with him. I felt like now I had a definite place to start being his mother. But I would feel awful if you thought that I was doing all this to punish you. Oh, Lisa, I'm sorry. I didn't mean for it to seem like I was keeping him away from you. But I guess in a way I have.''

I get the feeling Mom would like me to let her know it's okay to hug. But my head is all tangled up, full of knots that I can't pick apart. Only one little thread hangs loose anymore. The thread says, "Cody," and I grab on to it. "I want things the way they were.''

"What? What do you mean?''

"I want Cody to be the Commander again. He just gave up. That's not right.''

166

"Lisa, maybe he doesn't need to be the Commander anymore."

"No!"

"I promise not to keep him from you ever . . ."

"I want it to be the same as it was."

Mom looks down at her hands again. "You want me to stop being with Cody?"

I squirm in my place. The thread starts to slip away, starts to wind around itself. "No. That's not what I'm saying."

Mom's lower lip is starting to swell from where the coat-rack bashed it in against her teeth. It looks as if she's pouting.

I can't help it. My lower lip starts to tingle and I feel it growing straight out like Pinocchio's nose. Pretty soon we look like a pair of monkeys, upset because we haven't gotten our daily banana. "Cody was fine like he was. He was happy. He doesn't need to go to school." I just say it, but I don't know if I believe it anymore.

"I'm just going to have to ask you to take my word for it that he is learning. It will take a long time for anything to really show, but I've noticed a little difference myself. Honey, he's not just playing games with me. Mrs. Jenkins said he was crying when you took him away. Don't you think he wanted to stay, not just for play, but to work with her?"

"I don't know."

"Well," she sighs. "Think about this. What happens if we pull him from school? Make him stay home. Would you just as soon stay home? Not go to school? Never mind the classes you'd be missing. Think about the people."

I think of Van. Robert. Wondering if I'd have been better

off if I had never met either one of them. I don't answer.

"Lisa, it's sudden, what's happened with Cody. I should have thought more about you being part of the decisions for him, helping you adjust to his new schedule and needs. But I didn't. On the other hand it's happened, and he can't go back to the way he was." She points to the rack. "I think your bad luck with that thing showed you that much." She looks at me for the first time in a long while. Frowns. "What happened to your lip?"

"Nothing."

She hesitates at my answer. "Well . . . Lisa? Some of these things are hard to explain, but . . . Cody's been held back. Sure, he's been happy being the Commander, but that's only because we didn't try to make him be anything more. Who knows? Maybe he could be forming words by now."

"But being the Commander was great for him," I argue, still fighting with the tangles. But the thread with Cody is just a little ball. "He was a space explorer. He wasn't just a retarded kid," I finish. "He was somebody."

Then that voice comes back, coming from the center of the twisted nest where all my thoughts are caught and trying to get out, and it whispers to me, "Be somebody."

I remember Robert lying there, his lips faintly forming those awful words.

"I haven't kept Cody from growing," I say quietly, hoping she'll agree.

She answers, "I think we all have, honey. But it's nobody's fault. We didn't do it on purpose. And now we know what we've done wrong. We're correcting it. And . . . I

168

think at the same time you have to realize that he's kept you from growing, too."

"Hunh?" The nest explodes in a million pieces.

"Lisa, you've always been by his side. His playmate. You gave up all your other friends to be with him . . ."

"But I *wanted* to. He didn't make me. We had such a good time."

"I know. I know. But you did the same thing day after day. You didn't do anything more because Cody didn't demand it of you. And it would still be going on if not for our discoveries. For . . . how many years?"

My dumb exploded brain is empty. Like a blank movie screen. But somebody dims the lights and a film starts rolling. I see me, in the future, coming home from the community college every day to put a thirteen-year-old Cody under the coatrack. Only by that point he's practically wearing it like a hat because he's so big. And I . . . and I . . .

At eighteen, would I still be pushing Cody through the Mighty Mart on a broken-down stroller? Still arming him with the almighty cucumber to blast Zondarians?

What about my wanting to be an astronaut? Did that idea come out of pretending with Cody more than anything else? Do I want to be one just for him?

Mom is saying that, when I grow up, maybe I'll have to leave Cody behind.

But if I can't picture myself with him, where am I?

The voice whispers to me.

"Lisa?" Mom touches my head, I've been silent so long.

"Mom," I say, kind of softly, "Robert got beaten up bad in school today."

169

+13+

I tell Mom about the fight. Not about why I happened to be there, but everything else. After I'm done she calls the school, but no one she talks to seems to know a thing. "Worse than a hospital," she says, slamming down the phone. Then she calls Robert's home. The conversation on her end goes like this:

"Betty? Lisa . . . Yes. Yes, she's home. Uh-hunh, everything. Well, I don't know. No, I don't know. How is he? Uh-hunh. At the hospital?"

When she says "hospital" my stomach caves in.

"What can we do to help? Uh-hunh. Sure, I understand. That's probably all he needs. What? Well, I'm not sure." Mom looks out at me still sitting in the hallway. "I'll ask . . . What? Okay, if you're sure. Okay, if you're sure that's all right. Uh-hunh. Right. Bye."

Mom comes out and slides down beside me again. "He's doing fine."

"He's in the hospital?"

"No. He was there to be checked out, but he's home now. Mrs. Wormer invited us to come over. What do you think?"

I shrug. "I guess we should."

"Don't you want to?"

Who else will visit Robert if I don't? "Yes."

We have to wait for Dad to get home. Mom checks on Cody and then starts fixing dinner. I just lie on my bed, staring at the ceiling. After the movie projector ran out of film downstairs, my head went back to looking blank for a while. Now there are all sorts of people and places zooming across the screen. The guy in the booth has gone nuts and is trying to show twenty different movies at the same time, first ten seconds of one, then five seconds of another, seven seconds of a third. What I get is lots of bits and pieces.

But they're not movies. They're memories. Scenes about me, at all different ages. Only I can't really focus on any of them because they go by so fast. I suppose it's similar to when a person is about to die and has their whole life flash in front of their face. But I'm not dying. In fact, I feel like a baby. A dumb baby that's newly born and doesn't know a thing.

I hear Dad come home and I go downstairs. In the kitchen he's touching Mom's lip. "What happened to you?"

"The coatrack attacked me," she says, then lowers her head a little and looks out the corners of her eyes. That's her "I'll tell you all about it later" look.

So Dad just says, "Darn, I thought I'd gotten that thing trained properly by now." Mom gives him a weak smile.

171

He doesn't get a thing from me. He shrugs and goes upstairs.

He comes back down. "What happened to Cody's head?"

"He's fine," says Mom.

"But . . ."

"The coatrack got him, too."

Dad looks from me back to Mom. He throws up his arms. "Okay. Fine. Keep it a big secret." And flops down on a kitchen chair to read the evening paper. I don't blame him, I wouldn't believe her either.

After dinner Mom and I get ready to go. Mom tells Dad that we won't be gone long.

"Stay as long as you like," he says. "Cody and I will have a man-to-man talk. I'll find out what happened to his head." He smiles, trying to make fun of Mom.

"No, we can't stay late. Don't want to wear him out," says Mom.

"Wear him out? You're running somebody in a race?"

"No. We're going to visit a sick friend," she says.

"Can I ask who?"

"You may. We're going to the Wormers'. To see Robert."

"Robert's sick? What's he got?"

"Well . . . he's not sick . . . exactly."

"Not sick."

"No. He . . . he got hurt today."

Dad's teasing smile fades. He stares at Mom. Slowly, he turns toward the coatrack, then slowly turns back to us. "Forget it."

Poor Dad.

*

In the car we don't say much for the first mile or so. Then Mom asks, "So you went to get Cody right after the fight, hunh?"

"Yeah."

"You suppose one has anything to do with the other?"

I shrug.

"Maybe you should think about it, Lisa."

"I *am* thinking. It's all I've done this whole stupid afternoon." I put my head in my hand and lean against my window. I think Mom starts to say something more, but changes her mind.

Mrs. Wormer greets us at the door. She looks worn out.

"I'm glad you decided to come," she says after coming back from the closet. She doesn't ask us to go into the living room. Instead she keeps us standing in the hallway. "Either I'm pestering Robert about how he's feeling, or I'm down here not knowing what to do with myself."

"Isn't your husband home?"

"No . . . Robert senior is at the base."

So Robert is Wormer the Second, hunh? It figures they'd do that to him.

"How's he doing?" asks Mom.

"Okay, I think. We were worried there at the hospital about some of his teeth, but they're just a little loose. The doctor said they'll tighten up into place and he should just watch what he eats for a while." She heaves out a sigh and glances at me. "Lisa? Why don't you go on up? I'd like to talk a little with your mother."

No business about how impolite it is to have a young lady in his room this time. I look at Mom.

173

"Go ahead, honey. I'll see Robert later."

I wander up the dark stairs to a long hallway. There's light showing from only one of the rooms, so I figure that's got to be him. My knees a little shaky, I go on in.

He's not as bad as I imagined, which was dead. I thought maybe I'd find him laid out with his hands folded on his chest and a black rose sticking up in between them, Mrs. Wormer just too embarrassed to say anything after we'd gone to all the trouble to come over here. "I thought maybe she wouldn't notice," she'd tell my Mom, after I'd gone screaming out the front door.

He's sitting up in bed with the covers pulled to his chest. There's a white patch taped over one eye and cotton stuffed up both sides of his nose. His nose isn't in a splint so I guess it's not broken. Around his other eye is a lot of black and blue. In the center is a spot of brown, looking out at me.

"How are you?"

"Is my mom's car parked out front?"

"Yeah," I say, puzzled. I wonder if he's going to make a break for it. Get away from his parents, and me, once and for all.

"Well, go lie in the road and have her drive over you four or five times, then I'll ask you the same dumb question."

I look straight at the floor. If he doesn't want me as a friend anymore, then why have I bothered coming? Then I remember how Van pretended not to like me. I'm not going to do the same thing to him.

After I think about that it only takes me a few seconds before I forget I'm supposed to feel embarrassed. "Nice rug," I say, still looking down.

"My mom made it," he says indifferently. "She made it out of old flannel shirts of mine."

I realize that's the second time he's said "my mom," not "Robert's mom."

"Nice," I say again. The rag rug spirals out from the center into a nice oval shape. It's basically dark, but there is a wide variety of lighter colors in there, too.

That makes me start looking around at the rest of the room. He has nice shelves that, built out from the wall, frame his windows. There are photographs on them, a rock collection, bottles of different-colored glass. And lots of models — boats, tanks, race cars. No planes. There are some big models of monsters, including a werewolf, a mummy, Frankenstein, and one walking along with his head under his arm. His other arm is reaching out, as though he's going to grab somebody. But somewhere along the line Robert broke his fingers off. Now there's only the thumb, and it looks as if he's hitchhiking.

He has nice burgundy curtains that also look handmade. And I notice the lamp on his desk has matching cloth stretched over its shade. I look back at the rug. Burgundy is its main color, too. "Your mom did a nice job with your room."

Robert doesn't answer. He just starts making this clicking sound with his tongue. Like a clock, timing me. An alarm will probably go off when it's time for me to leave.

His eye isn't looking at me anymore. With all the bandages and stuff it seems as though that's all that's left of him. A roaring bonfire that's dwindled to one little shining coal. If I'm not careful, maybe it will go out. Then there will never be any more kings, or generals, or presidents coming out of him. There won't even be any Robert.

I look away quickly, searching for something else to talk about that's in his room.

When I see it, my blood stops. The red corpuscles say "Whoa!" and put on the brakes. My heart is confused and sends up a message to my brain. "What's the holdup?" My brain is busy elsewhere. It's telling my eyes to make the thing in front of them disappear.

My voice sneaks out of my throat, dry as sand. "You have a television."

The ticking stops. Robert has wound down. My time is up. But there's no alarm. Only his voice saying, "I've got cable. Twenty-six stations."

I whirl on him. "How can you have a television?"

"When my parents got a new one, they gave me the old."

"No. You don't understand." Forgetting all the manners my mother taught me to use around an unwell person, I rush up to the head of his bed and bend my whole face down toward that eyeball of his. I can't believe it. "No A.T.B.R. at all."

The back of Robert's head turns into a shovel. It starts digging into his pillow. "Hunh?"

"How long have you watched . . . that thing?"

"That particular one?"

"No! No! During your *life*."

"Since I was little. I don't know. What's going on?"

I groan and slump down onto the edge of his bed. My theory is ruined. Robert, the most creative person I've ever met, watches television. That means it hasn't killed off the brain cells of kids in school. And Cody is just an unusual kid who happens not to like it. I should have figured something was wrong, I guess, as soon as Robert started doing *Let's Make a Deal* so well. "I don't feel too good. Is there room enough under the covers for me?"

Of course I don't mean it, but Robert goes, "No!" His one eye is not enough to express all the surprise that's inside of him. It keeps trying to open wider to make up for the other eye that isn't there, but he just can't do it. "I'm in my *pajamas*," he hisses.

I have to laugh. Robert Wormer? Shy about something? Who'd ever have thought it? Then I remember that I don't know Robert Wormer. I only know Lord So-and-So, Prince This-and-That. But Robert Wormer, he's an unknown commodity, someone I've really only talked to once or twice.

"Who is Robert Wormer?" I ask.

"What?"

"You heard me. Who *are* you?"

But the eye wanders away from me. It gets small, very small. I see it trying not to get hit again, trying not to get hurt. Trying to avoid the punches that all the great people who ever lived in the world couldn't stop. I decide I'd better go.

"I'll be back," I say from the door. Robert closes his eye.

Mom and Mrs. Wormer look up when I appear, then stand. "I guess we better leave," says Mom.

"Can't I get you anything to eat? Drink?" asks Mrs. Wormer.

"Cookies and milk?" I think.

"No thanks," says Mom. "I have to go home and

177

straighten out somebody about a coatrack.'' Mrs. Wormer looks at her curiously but doesn't ask any questions. "I'll just run up and say hello to Robert."

Mom disappears upstairs, leaving me and Mrs. Wormer alone with nothing to say.

"He looks kind of gruesome, doesn't he?" she asks.

I nod. "I don't know if he was glad to see me or not."

"Oh, I'm sure he was. He's always liked you so much," says Mrs. Wormer.

I look up at her, surprised. But why should I be surprised? Before my bad day in Mrs. Cronski's class, Robert liked me a lot. But then I think, "Didn't he?" He kissed me all those times, and I was never sure what it meant.

"Robert hasn't been very happy for several years now. I was hoping a good friend, like you, might change him."

I almost say, "What do you mean? He used to be happy all the time." Instead I shake my head. "He changed me."

Now it's her turn to be surprised. "Oh?"

"He took me to faraway countries. Made me a queen. And even though those things weren't real, I never had anyone before think I was worth taking to places like that, or who could imagine somebody like me being those people. Until Robert."

When she says, "That's sweet," I could strangle myself for having told her. But then she says, "It hurt him, though, didn't it?"

All of a sudden I'm looking down at another rug made by her and not answering.

"Robert used to have a lot of different interests. But he gave them up. He had a lot of good ideas, too. I'm not sure what happened. But he just doesn't hang on to his ideas anymore. He hasn't been happy since.''

I stare at her. Is she saying that, though he could whisk us off to anywhere in the world, he wasn't really happy?

"But he was happy," I insist. "His first few months at school, at least.''

"Are you sure?''

"Yes.''

"Did you ask him? Did Robert tell you himself that he was happy?''

No. I never asked Robert. Robert was never there to ask. When he did talk about himself, it was mostly to complain about his parents. Does that mean that, even while he was having fun with me, he was still angry deep down inside? I sigh. If I didn't even know how he felt about me, how would I know how he felt about himself?

"Did *you* ever ask him?" I say.

"No. It was obvious to me." She sounds pretty sure.

"Maybe," I begin slowly, "even if it was obvious, you should have asked him anyway.''

She thinks about that and nods. "Asked *something*, at least. Considering what happened today. But I kept waiting for Robert, all by himself, to change back to the way he was.''

The way he was? I shake my head when I hear that. "You think that he liked everything okay when he was a lot younger?''

"Of course," she says.

"Then why would he have wanted to start messing around, making you mad?" When she doesn't answer I say,

"You never asked him if he was happy when you thought he wasn't. Did you ever ask him when you thought he was? Just to check? Just to make sure?"

Mrs. Wormer's mouth opens a little, but not to speak to me. It opens the way it sometimes does when a person thinks hard, when they have to talk seriously to themselves.

When Mom comes down we say some encouraging words about Robert healing quickly, and then get in the car.

On the way home I start thinking again about the day and everything that's happened and everything that people have said. Mostly I think about Robert. How if his parents had talked to him, found out what he was thinking instead of just expecting him to act the way he was told, things could have been different for him. How if he'd just been allowed to be himself he never would have gotten into trouble, never have gotten beat up. How, even though I had a good time meeting all his people, maybe I'd have had a better time meeting *him*.

"Robert liked to pretend even more than Cody," I say out loud.

"Maybe that's why you became his friend. Maybe he reminded you of that part of Cody," says Mom.

I think about Cody not being the Commander anymore and starting to grow up, and how Robert, in his own way, didn't stop being the Commander, using school as his Zondar. His mom said he used to have lots of ideas but he gave up on them. What were they? What wonderful things could he have told me about if he hadn't been so busy hiding inside other people? I want to know. Mom says we stopped

180

Cody from growing. Robert's parents did the same thing to him. I can hear his mom's voice in my head, worried about him, and I can still picture all the care she put into his room. Caring isn't enough, I guess. I cared for Cody.

I remember the jar of wheat Dad brought home, the batch that failed. Despite everything all those scientists did, despite all the good things they put into the seeds, they still didn't grow. Maybe that happens with families too. Like mine and Robert's. So much good stuff was poured in, but some of us still went haywire. And, like my mom said, it's nobody's fault. It just happens.

"I think I was scared," I say to Mom.

She looks over from driving. "Scared? When?"

"Today. At school. I thought Robert could do anything, because he never let people intimidate him. I thought he was brave. A lot braver than me. And invulnerable. Then when he started getting in trouble because he thought I'd . . . let him down, I think I began to wonder, in the back of my head, if all that was really true. I didn't intimidate him, but I hurt him in a way. When Jimmy Pinto knocked him down, that showed me he wasn't a real-life Superman. His Superman was part of the make-believe, too. And I got scared. It was like Robert had lied to me."

"And Cody's never lied to you," offers Mom.

"No. He's always been himself with me. But . . . but then I tried to make him not be himself. I wanted him to be somebody else, the old Cody, the one I used to know but isn't around anymore. Because I thought then I'd be safe, and everything would be all right again. Pretty selfish, hunh?"

"But understandable, I think."

When we get in the driveway and Mom turns off the motor, we sit for a while longer.

"Mom? You think Robert will get better? I mean, will he go back to school and start it all over again?"

"Do you think he will?"

I think about Robert's eye, getting small and frightened. "No. But if he can't be himself, and he can't be other people, what's left?"

"What's left are friends. And family. To help him decide on an answer. Also, I mentioned Dr. Barnes to Mrs. Wormer. Will you get mad at me for that?"

I shake my head.

She opens her door. The little interior light comes on. Her face looks very tired.

"You look tired," she says to me. I laugh. "What's so funny?"

"I was just thinking that there've been days when I've seen *you* looking a lot better," I say.

"That bad, hunh? Well, let me go clear up things with your father and then we'll all get to bed early."

We tromp up the front steps, two tired zombies. Maybe Mrs. Jenkins would believe me now.

Inside the house, I notice right away that something is missing. It isn't until we get into the living room that I find out what it is.

Dad is standing there, ready for us. He's holding a leash that runs down to the floor and attaches to a collar that's

182

around the neck of the coatrack, lying on its side. The face of a dog has been drawn on a piece of paper and taped to the ball, and cardboard ears are sticking straight up.

"What have you . . ."

Dad holds up his hand, cutting off Mom. "I've spent a grueling time here while you've been gone, trying to straighten this beast out. Now pay attention." He talks to the rack. "Okay, Peanut . . ."

"Peanut?"

"Please, he's very sensitive about his name. Peanut . . . play dead." Dad gives the rack a little poke with his foot and it rolls over on its side. "Attaboy. All right. Peanut, sit up." Dad hauls the rack upright by the leash. "Very good. Very good indeed. Now, for his final feat . . . Peanut, speak."

Nothing happens.

"Peanut. Don't let me down. Speak."

Nothing.

Dad clears his throat and looks at us apologetically. "Really, we've been working quite hard on this performance. Maybe he just . . ."

Abruptly, we hear barking. Barking that sounds very much like a five-year-old boy who's underneath all the coats and hats that have been piled on the sofa.

"Peanut! You came through. Good boy." Dad pats the rack on the head. "I hereby declare this coatrack safe and noncarnivorous. All he needs to keep him happy is a few kind words every morning, thanking him for holding all our outdoor clothes for us overnight. Thank you, Peanut."

Mom goes and gives Dad a big hug. I dig Cody out from

183

the pile on the sofa. "Pazzuh!" he goes when he sees me.

"Why do I get shot?" I ask.

Dad, one arm around Mom, one around Peanut, says, "For not realizing that coatracks have feelings too."

I smile. Here, at least, everything's back to normal.

◆14◆

I visit Robert several times after that. He still never says much, although I think he's glad to see me. When he's better his mom has a special conference with Mr. Mann, who had expelled Robert because of the fight. Colonel Wormer couldn't make it. It takes about two minutes of Mrs. Wormer's finger for Mr. Mann to decide to let Robert back in.

When Robert reappears in school, he goes back to being the same old Robert, but toned down a lot. He doesn't act up in class anymore or stand up in the middle of assemblies. And he's one person now: Wormer the Wondrous. He has started wearing a top hat and cape. You can usually find him out in the school commons, keeping kids bug-eyed by making coins vanish into thin air or levitating somebody's math book. Mom says he's seeing Dr. Barnes along with his mother.

He smiles at me in the hall, and that's about it. He

doesn't ignore me, but he doesn't try to take me to exotic places, either. It's a nice smile, though.

Jimmy Pinto is still around, but quieter. He doesn't seem to be terrorizing the school as much as he used to. Maybe Robert did get in a few hits of his own, in a way.

Van and I are friends again, but we don't hang out together the way we used to. She's still making speeches.

I go in and listen one day, sitting in the back row again. The crowd is about the same size. Mr. Mann is there. His head has dropped forward and I can hear soft snores. But the cheerleaders are gone. Marcia Tyler's dating the quarterback now.

In her speech Van's still down on boys, but at least she doesn't refer to them as fires or floods or other natural disasters this time. At the end of it Robert, who's been sitting in the front row but off to the side, goes over to the stage, takes off his hat, pulls out a flower, and hands it to her before walking away. I can't be sure from this distance, but I think she's blushing.

Van's started a new fashion trend. She's taken her dad's sweaters and altered them. She wears them as dresses, with a slip on underneath instead of her torn T-shirt and pants. She's letting her green hair grow out. To hide the dark roots she wears colorful scarves around her head, making the rest of her hair sprout out the top. She looks like a carrot. An interesting carrot. Already I've seen two other girls imitating her.

I think she's losing weight.

All of a sudden people seem to want to talk to me. I guess they did before, but I was always too busy with Van or Robert to notice. They think it's neat that I know two of the most flamboyant kids in school. They also think I have a great sense of humor. Me! They remember my acting days with Robert in the cafeteria and tell me what a riot I was. Me! Not Robert, but me! I guess television doesn't do any harm after all.

I've met Dr. Barnes. He's not at all what I expected. He doesn't wear a white suit and work in an antiseptic room that has straitjackets and giant hypodermics hanging on the walls. He has an office like somebody's living room, with plants and sofas and a coffee table, and he's usually dressed like my dad, only his shirt doesn't hang out. The whole family goes and we sit around and talk. Sometimes he has ideas for us to work on at home. Other times he just sits and ̶ ̶ ̶ to how things are going, gets concerned if we have a ̶ ̶m, gets excited when something good has happened. One time I tell him, "Dr. Barnes, you're not much like a doctor. You're more like a good friend."

He smiles at me. "Thanks. That's what I try to be. I used to be an aardvark." His main problem is he gets a little strange when he tries to be funny.

Mom and I have worked it out so that we both help Cody after school. She concentrates on one area with him, I concentrate on another. A lot of the time it doesn't seem as though we're getting anywhere at all with him. But that's okay, because then Mom and I can encourage each other to keep going. Other times, when he has a particularly good day, we celebrate together. Dad is content just to be in there sometimes with us. If Cody gets frustrated with Mom and me, he'll run to Dad, and Dad loves it.

"Your teachers driving you crazy again? Well, just sit here with me a while."

When we complain to him that we're not done, Dad snarls and waves an imaginary sword at us to keep us at bay. Cody eats it up.

They're also letting me do chores around the house again the way I used to. Dr. Barnes calls what my parents did a "flip-flop." Meaning that since they felt guilty about my having had to do so much on my own they turned around and stopped letting me do *anything*. Grownups definitely have strange problems. I'm not sure I'm going to like being one.

The coatrack is back in the hall. It doesn't fly into space anymore and go on adventures. It's just a coatrack. Sometimes I'll find Dad patting it on the head in the morning as he's going out the door. His idea must be working bitten anybody in weeks.